SHAARA – BEGINNINGS AND ENDINGS

Book 5 of The Shaarvan Series

Note: To start at the beginning of this series, please go to *Scholar-Ship-Bound.*

K.S. Riggin

Table of Contents

Main Characters & Places in the Shaarvan Series

Altar: Home of the Shapechanger & others. Altar is both the name of the planet and the capital city.

Altarian: One who lives on Altar.

Baltoff: The Old One on Westla who was manufacturing the drugs that Thenos used to overthrow the government of Altar.

Barquel: The main god worshipped on Freinana

Blair: Owner of the Landoor ranch. Good guy.

Brala: Shaara's friend on Westla

Chaslow: Shapechanger working for Thenos, blew up the nursery on Westla & hunted for Shaara.

Clofa: One of Altar's two moons. It was where the old Shapechanger liked to retire. Thenos blew it up.

Crimson Black: The horse-like landoor Shaara befriends

Flar: Freinana housemaster that Shaara stays with. Husband of Frieda

Frieda: Freinana housemistress that Shaara stays with. Wife of Flar

Goria: Pseudo wife of Pathe. Former lover of Shaarvan. Bad person

Isandor: The Commoner who owns Shaara on Freinana. Bad guy

Landoor: Animal that looks like a horse

Pathe: Son of Tevor & Teea (brother of Shaarvan & Thenos) Doctor, good guy

Saberey: Symbol of the Shapechanger & their origin

Shaara: College student. Wife of Shaarvan and later Stegthal (Thal) Renamed numerous times: Susan, Sletttha, Sleena, Skeva, Thalia, Thenosa

Shaarac: (Thaarac, Thenon) Shaara and Shaarvan's son

Shaarvan: Steals his wife, Shaara, from a college campus, Altarian Shapechanger

Skeva: Name given to Shaara on Freinana

Sleena: Name given to Shaara on Freinana
Slettha: Slaver's name for Shaara on Freinana
Spelon: One of Shaara's guardians. Shapechanger Warrior, becomes Shaara's lover later
Stegthal: (Thal) He becomes Shaara's Second Husband. Good & bad
Susan: Shaara's original Earth name
Targone: Shapechanger who arrives on Freinana to verify that Shaara is Shapechanger
Teea: Shaarvan's mother, lives on Altar, wife of Tevor (and later Starnkor)
Tem: Head of Westla, Uncle to Shaarvan, Tevor's brother
Temina: Wife of Tem, mentally unstable
Tenor: One of Shaara's guardians. Shapechanger Warrior
Tessa: High Priestess
Tevor: Shaarvan's father, lives on Altar, husband of Teea
Thal: Stegthal's name on Deathstar
Thalia: Shaara's name on Deathstar
Thandar: Shaara & Thal's son. Shaarvan adopts him. He becomes Shaandar.
Thedar: One of Shaara's guardians. Shapechanger Warrior
Theinian: Another species, usually slavers and most often gay
Thenos: Son of Tevor & Teea (brother of Shaarvan & Pathe) Bad guy
Tren: Owner of the casino and of Shaara. Good guy to Shaara
Westla: Huge artificial satellite. Only Shapechanger may go there or girls and servants

Additional Terminology:

Tide: Approximately one Earth Tide. Tides are usually grouped, as in a fiveTide, twentyTide, etc.

Pass: Approximately one year. A halfPass and quarterPass are common expressions.

Shapechanger: Never found in the plural. The Shapechanger are an artificially derived species that are capable of shape change, most often as a Saberey (tiger-like cat), This also includes many sensory improvements and abilities.

The Names of Shapechanger: Names beginning with T or S denote Power. Those Shapechanger are deemed Lords. Formal testing on Westla ranks them.

Warrior Shapechanger: Those who meet qualifications of specific battle readiness. Ranking is by formal tests on Westla.

Priestess: Females who have achieved a ranking on Westla denoting their ability to stand up against Shapechanger Power.

Prelude

Shaara on the artificial planet, Westla

Years ago, I was a college student in Los Angeles. An interview for a scholarship brought no scholarship, only a one-way ticket into space. I'd fought my capture, but against my will my husband altered, impregnated, and trained me to Shapechanger standards. I didn't accept Shapechanger beliefs, but acceptance wasn't mandatory, while obedience was. My rocky Shapechanger transition, including a stay on a planet called Freinana, where I'd been a mere slave, had mellowed my rebellions.

I loved Shaarvan and the son we'd created, but life was never placid. My husband, Shaarvan, had just left me on the massive artificial satellite Westla to fly back to Altar, the planet where his parents lived. Before his ship lifted up, he'd given me to a strange Shapechanger named Stegthal, one who was now supposed to be my Second, whatever that meant.

Like a book discarded, passed to someone else to read and enjoy, I was supposed to just go along with it. And what made it even worse, my bondmates, the other three huge Shapechanger Warriors my husband had bonded me to, all went along with the arrangement. So, there I was, stuck on an alien space station/planet, alone and helpless, except for my rage.

Chapter One

Shaara on the artificial planet, Westla

My husband's ship had just lifted up and disappeared through the great Saberey eye of Westla. I had no idea when Shaarvan would return. My grief was beyond hysteria, somewhat just shy of the Kingdom of Madness. I know that sounds extreme, but Shaarvan and I were bonded in the Saberey Forests, in a soul bond much deeper than anything on Earth. We communed by thoughts and shared an affinity that, although it was new and still being forged, had created the backbone of my existence. Its absence was like undergoing the extraction of an organ. (Perhaps my lungs, because I could barely breathe.)

The Shapechanger males who walked beside me remained calm, as if the wrench of my life force was nothing. In fact, if the scents around me were correct, the stale odor of pampa fruit, accompanied by its faint yellow haze, indicated that they were irritated by my expressions of anguish. Spelon, as always, reeked of mustard, the aroma of battle readiness, but that was nothing new. He probably bathed in the fragrance.

The hall where we walked felt empty. Where had all the couples gone? Normally, solitary males rushed about, intent on their mysterious errands. Why didn't I see any of them this Tide? My eyes searched, but only walls — stark-white and passageway-tight, stretched out ahead. Like parallel lines, they leaned increasingly inward. The distant, narrowed end looked to be the sole path ahead.

Stegthal pressed in too closely at my right, his arm in constant contact with me. I knew him the least of my guardians. The War Lord was lithe and tall, towering even above Thedar. Like all Shapechanger, Stegthal was handsome, heavily muscled from the strict regime of weapons work that they all practiced. He was supposed to be super smart, at least according to Shaarvan. A scientist, my husband had told me. I'd already felt Stegthal's Power at my testing. I knew he was the strongest of the Warrior Shapechanger, strongest, at least in Shapechanger Mind Force.

The three other males who cocooned about me with their huge, heavy bodies had spent time with me, taking me on interesting and sometimes fun jaunts about Westla. I felt slightly easier with each of them. Less pressured, anyway. They laughed and seemed, if not human, at least friendly. But even so, at the moment, I felt imprisoned by their proximity, smothered in their mountains of testosterone.

My testing in the Court Arena had supposedly granted me some freedom. I could meet the eyes of males and speak more freely in social situations. I could even touch my guardians. But my guardians were still stronger physically and stronger in Power than I was. Equality was not on the horizon.

The tread of the males' wood-hard heels produced the only sound in the empty hall. The steady beat of it reminded me of military drills or parades, but the stance of the males was far too alert for a casual march. Each of them was battle-ready, although only Spelon harbored the smell of it.

My eyes began to watch the rhythm of their feet. Like some multi-legged insect, the progression of their limbs stepping together, moving forward, and then together again fascinated me — clump thump, clump thump, right-left, right-left.

I stretched out my legs to expand their reach. My pace could almost match theirs for a moment, but I couldn't keep it up for long. I hop-skipped a stride as I lost the beat. Immediately, the males slowed their pace, although they said nothing. Did they realize that my shorter legs made me slower, or did they believe me to be a dawdler?

Shaarvan had forced me to wear dainty, delicate lavender slippers that Tide. The shoes made me even more slow than usual. The shoe's elegance was in honor of my Second Wedding, a wedding that had been forced on me that morning.

My slippers glittered with their many-faceted tiny pieces of glass. In the lights of the great passageway, they were very pretty, but for walking, they were soft-soled marshmallows. Like the lavender gown I wore, my shoes only served the purpose of making me pleasingly feminine by Shapechanger standards. I sighed and laughed at myself. Restrictive shoes and trippingly long gowns were the least of my concerns.

My mind darted back to that farce of a wedding. I'd been married to Shaarvan for more than two Passes, yet he'd forced me to marry another, a Second husband. I'd been told that it was often done on Westla, the metallic and artificial planet I currently lived on. It meant that if Shaarvan should be killed in the war on Altar, I'd belong to my Second husband, Stegthal. However, although I'd obeyed Shaarvan's will in the wedding ceremony, I knew that if Shaarvan were really to die, I would not continue to live and be Stegthal's. I would not want to.

Yet, this Shapechanger beside me, because of one short, empty ceremony, believed he had the right to my obedience. I hated his claim on me, and I resented him. He, a stranger to me, except in the eyes of the law, had wrapped his arms about me at Spaceport and kept me from running after my love. I'd fought Stegthal, monster that he was, but he'd ignored my pleas. He'd held me back as Shaarvan walked up the ship's ramp, and my Second hadn't loosened his prisoner's hold on me until Shaarvan's ship lifted up through the eye of the Saberey.

I'd despised Stegthal even before the ceremony, but it was a tiny flame of loathing compared with how I felt after Shaarvan's ship became nothing more than a flash of metal in the cold, dark sky. When I could no longer see the brightness of the faint star that was the ship journeying away from me, then like a child so confused he turns to an enemy for consolation, my hands and arms had clung to Stegthal, and I'd wet his shirt with my tears. I, who owned only my pride, had given it to this alien Lord. How could I help but abhor Stegthal?

Without my willing it, my eyes shot up to the male Shaarvan had forced on me. Stegthal was officially a bondmate, like the other three males, but the others had spent time with me. Thedar and Tenor were kind of friends, or maybe brothers? I shivered thinking about Spelon.

I was glad Shaarvan had not made Spelon my Second. Yet, Shaarvan placed Spelon next in succession. If Stegthal were to die, Spelon would become my Second. Why? Why Stegthal and Spelon? Why couldn't Shaarvan have left me under Thedar's care or Tenor's? Why did he choose the two males I feared the most?

Stegthal caught my glance. He smiled down at me. I dropped my eyes and kept them lowered, but I felt the intensity of Stegthal's gaze on me for several moments. Beneath his probe, I fidgeted. Again, my legs stretched out, and I walked a little faster.

Spelon snorted a laugh. "Have you decided to walk instead of crawl?"

I didn't respond. For a time, I ignored the pain in the heel of my left foot. A blister was forming, but if I mentioned it, Stegthal would probably insist on carrying me. I couldn't endure his touch again.

I shot another glance upwards when I felt Stegthal look away. All I'd noticed before about him was his height. I studied my Second, attempting to analyze the lines of his face. Perhaps that would hint at his nature.

His face was smooth, free from the small bristly hairs that marred the chins of men on my home planet, Earth. But that was true of all Shapechanger. They were genetically engineered in a way the bio-scientists had long ago chosen. More or less perfection, except for one fault, which kept them from producing female children. Thus, I and all the other females were products of alien worlds.

Another peek upward — Stegthal carried no frown lines or age lines that would hint at his character. The sharp planes of cheekbones, far too high and clearly defined to be other than Shapechanger, spoke to me of an unbending nature. So he was stubborn, decisive, and domineering. What else was new?

Stegthal's dark hair, almost black and straight as the fall of a cascade, kept tumbling into his eyes. It only partially hid the thickness of his heavy brows. The hand that raked it upwards was long and broad. Strong hands.

Stegthal shot another glance down at me. I stumbled. Spelon, on my left, reached out and gripped my arm. The pain of his overly tight hold made me cry out. I jerked away.

I hardly saw the look that passed from Stegthal to Spelon, yet I felt the angry currents in the air. I didn't need to see Stegthal's territorial glower. I'd been around Shapechanger males long enough to know that Stegthal had warned off Spelon.

Angrily, I stamped forward more briskly. Darn Shaarvan for giving me to this arrogant stranger. It wasn't like Spelon had attempted to steal me away. All Spelon had tried to do was keep me from falling. And I wasn't Stegthal's anyway. What right did he have to be jealous?

I didn't like Spelon, but at least I understood him. He was simply a chauvinistic jerk. I could deal with him by offering a couple of smiles, downcast eyes, and the act I put on, pretending I was humble and submissively feminine. I hoped such simple methods would work on Stegthal.

Once again, Stegthal's eyes were watching me. I looked away, but not before I'd seen that he was laughing at me. Had he been reading my thoughts? How could he? Of course, Shaarvan could, but that was different. He and I were deeply bonded.

I stole another peek upwards. Stegthal's eyes were still on me, amused and fully knowledgeable. He *was* reading my thoughts. My face grew hot, and my anger boiled. I concentrated with renewed determination on walking faster, but the pain in my left heel was becoming harder to shut out.

Stegthal's hand reached out and halted me. His grip on my arm wasn't painful like Spelon's, but it was forceful. I knew I couldn't shake it off. I raised my eyes and met his. I could feel the currents of Shapechanger Power, like soundwaves, except solid, physical. The strength of it surprised me. I'd known Stegthal held a high rank. All of my bondmates did. Shaarvan had chosen the highest of the Warlords, but I could tell that Stegthal's Power was nearer to Tem's, Shaarvan's uncle and head of Westla.

"You are in pain, Child. Where are you hurt?" Stegthal asked with a gentleness I hadn't expected.

I did not want his gentleness nor his sympathy. I lashed out. "My husband has left me, and you ask that?"

I used his surprise at my reply to pull away.

Spelon, standing a bit further away than he had before, whistled under his breath. Then, he whispered loudly to Thedar, "I bet eleven difras Shaara doesn't make it home without a beating,"

I glared at Spelon, but I saw the way Thedar and Tenor were looking at me. Their eyes cautioned. My glance shot back to Stegthal. Darkened eyes, tight jaw, a hint of tiger markings. Danger.

I dropped my chin and studied the fake stone pattern on the ground. "Forgive me," I said. I supposed I should offer more, but my mind went dead. I counted stones and listened to the silence.

Spelon shifted. The leather of his vest rustled. I didn't move. My eyes still contemplated the appearance of the pathway.

I could feel the anger. Like a fierce hot wind, it buffeted me. Rotten pampa fruit, the odor of garbage, assailed me for a moment. I knew the feel and smell of male displeasure. I'd felt it often. I didn't cower from it, but I didn't dare look up and meet Stegthal's eyes.

He was considering punishment. My mind began to analyze his movements. First, he leaned slightly towards me. His feet balanced and absorbing the movement, shifting their stance like a cat preparing to pounce. Then his hand slowly lifted. The hand rose too slowly to deliver a slap, yet I knew the danger was not over. He took a half step toward me. Again, his balance shifted. I didn't move. I could barely breathe as his hand moved forward to cup my chin and bring my face up to look at him.

"Answer me, Child," he said, in a voice mild as a ticking time bomb.

Again, the leather of Spelon's vest crinkled as he stirred. Thedar coughed as if to clear his throat. My heart raced.

"Unless you want Spelon to win his bet," Stegthal added as my silence continued.

The question? What had he asked me? My mind panicked until I remembered. "My heel is sore," I whispered, hoping I would not get caught in a Shapechanger lie. A sore was thankfully close enough to a blister to get by. I felt only a tinge of nausea, not the upset a real lie would have caused. I breathed shallowly, still waiting for the reprimand.

Stegthal watched me fixedly. My eyes darted a glance. His were like storm clouds, yet he did not chastise, although. I could tell he knew there was more to it than I'd said.

"I shall carry you if you wish," he offered, with a voice that held no evidence of having taken offense at my behavior.

"No!" I blurted out, so horrified by his offer I forgot my fear.

Once more, the feel of Stegthal's disapproval warned me. The dry heat of its contact against my skin made me soften my reply.

"Thank you, my Lord," I added.

Again, his eyes flashed, not in anger, this time, but with something else. The faint scent of gardenias mixed with cherry blossoms tickled my nose. I'd never registered that odor before. I sought for meaning. My Shapechanger senses caught me up. Amusement.

For a moment, Stegthal held my chin and studied me. The strength of his Power surrounded me, enveloping me with the feel of it. The flower scent wafted away, replaced by something stranger, something unidentifiable, something frightening. I began to shiver like a shaken molded pudding dessert.

The winds halted, sucked back inside him, but an almost static-electric residue teased my skin.

Had I angered him so much that he'd almost used his Power on me? Or had it been just for show? Either way, my lowered eyes were no act. My legs barely supported me. I had a sudden urge to pee. I breathed in deeply and attempted to regain some courage.

To be touched by so much Shapechanger force was like being pushed off a cliff and then rescued at the moment just before you hit the ground. Stegthal hadn't hurt me, but he'd alerted me to the danger of challenging him.

He released my chin and nodded. "All right, Child, walk if you can."

Like a zombie, I staggered on, my mind reeling. Shaarvan had never handled me like that. Shapechanger did not believe in forcing others with Power and almost never blanketed anyone with it, yet Stegthal had. Why? Why would he break with tradition? Why had my bondmates allowed it? Surely, they'd felt it, too?

I had slowed again, but no one mentioned it. Surprisingly, Spelon remained noticeably quiet. Even Stegthal had released his grip, which was good because my skin felt raw and hyper-sensitive. Close proximity to that amount of Power prickled irritatingly.

I tried not to think about what Stegthal had done. I concentrated instead on placing my foot down and walking without any noticeable limp. I found that if I stepped slightly on the side, the blister didn't hurt as much. Another step, breathe, another step, breathe. I didn't know where we were going or how much longer I would need to keep walking, but I knew that I must. Step, breathe, step, breathe . . .

I started thinking about the look I'd seen in Stegthal's eyes just after he'd withdrawn his Power. It had almost seemed compassionate — not something Shapechanger were known for. And could someone with that much Power ever feel empathy?

As much as I hated him, I had to admit that Stegthal had been patient with me. When Shaarvan's ship had left, I'd gone crazy. My screams had pierced the air and probably Stegthal's ears, but he hadn't silenced me. My writhing body had struck and kicked him, my arms flailing about like the unhinged blades of a windmill. Yet, throughout it, Stegthal had kept his temper. Spelon wouldn't have. He would have knocked me out with his fist. Thedar and Tenor would have used the neck grip. Shaarvan would have . . .

That one stray thought stripped me of the last shreds of my composure. I whimpered a high-pitched wail of agony, my foot turned, and I landed fully on the blister. With the double onslaught of pain, I stumbled, one breath from collapse. Stegthal's arms swept me up.

"Don't touch me!" I screamed.

"Behave." The word was a slap. No warmth, no compassion.

His touch nauseated. It felt vile and repulsive, yet I froze, having the good sense not to resist. "I'm sorry," I uttered automatically.

When we arrived at the next intersection, I gained the courage to peek at my other bondmates. Thedar was busy scanning the corridors that branched each side. Tenor was looking backward as if he thought an enemy might creep up from behind. Spelon, who usually acted as the Warrior of the group, was not playing *lookout*. His eyes were burning into mine. He looked angry.

I knew this intersection. I could feel the proximity of Shaarvan's chambers. All the passageways were alike, and only the eyes of the males could read the color-coding at the bottom of the walls, but I felt it, like a calling inside me — *Home, home, home*, it said.

Everything would be fine once we were home. The pain in my heart lifted. Like a sunflower, my face turned toward the dwelling, yet Stegthal kept walking.

"My quarters are there," I said, pointing to the door.

"Yes, those are Shaarvan's quarters, Child, but he is gone. You no longer live there. You live with me now."

"Thedar, Tenor," I called out, but my bondmates shook their heads. "Spelon," I pleaded.

"He is your Second, Shaara. You must live with him." Spelon's voice was a growl of anger. I could barely understand the words.

"No. Shaarvan didn't tell me that. He would have told me if he wanted me to move. He won't know where I am. How will he find me?"

"He will always find you. You know that," Stegthal said, clamping me more firmly to his chest.

It was not until we reached the doorstep of a farther dwelling that Stegthal stopped. I felt him palm the frontal, and then he carried me inside.

"This will be your home now," Stegthal said as he set me down in a chair.

I felt dizzy. I could barely take in my new surroundings. The huge bodies of my bondmates were crowding in on me.

"Tenor, Spelon, Thedar. I can't stay here. Please." I tried to make eye contact, pleading for understanding. Even Spelon, Warrior of the Shapechanger, focused his eyes upward, refusing my plea.

I glanced about — same white walls, same food machines, similar table and chairs. There was not really any difference from Shaarvan's residence, but yet, Stegthal's felt wrong. It socked me in the stomach and forced tears from eyes, too dry to cry anymore.

I scanned my guardians' faces, searching for a hint of their thoughts. None of them took me seriously. Even in my mind, I could hear the echo of my sobs, my behavior at the Spaceport, the childish way I'd ignored all Shapechanger training.

I drew in a measured breath and pushed down my anger then formed my thoughts into bubbles of stillness as Tessa had taught me. I concentrated on only the matter of my place of residence. Then I took an even deeper breath and said, "Please, it is important . . ."

Stegthal let out a chuckle that broke into my sentence. "I welcome your composure, Child, but I will not hear your arguments. The decision is final. You will not return to your former chambers, not while Shaarvan is away — not as long as you are my responsibility."

I glared at all of them. How could they think I could live with a strange male while I waited for my husband's return?

Hard gray eyes viewed me. All of them with stern faces — grim-faced, impassive, and set. Tessa was right — males *did* have rocks for hearts.

The chair had begun its adjustments to accommodate my size and weight. I was used to the wiggle, like a live animal vibrating beneath me. But then a tinny, robotic voice from deep inside it announced, "Body restoration required."

Stegthal, in the process of pushing buttons to bring up chairs for the bondmates, stopped. "Shaara?" he said, but he strode towards me without finishing his thought. He ripped off both shoes and examined my feet.

"Stupidity," he growled.

A yellow mist, accompanied by the scent of anger — rotten pampa fruit — burst into the air, first from Stegthal, then Spelon. How interesting I could identify the individual flavors. But as I was contemplating that, Stegthal's thoughts seeped into mine.

I should have known, should have seen her pain. What kind of husband does not feel the injuries of his wife?

Thedar handed Stegthal some medicine. He took it and gently soothed away the blister's pain. My heel was bleeding, but it was far less serious than my injuries on Freinana, most of which I'd ignored. Besides, I was thinking more about Stegthal's thoughts than about troubling over a silly little blister.

Stegthal finished doctoring me. I thanked him as he straightened up. He nodded at me, but he and Thedar were talking in some language I had not yet learned. Whatever they were speaking about, neither looked happy.

I looked about the room. If it was to be my new prison, I figured it would be wise to become acquainted.

We were sitting in the eating room with the traditional Westlan kidney-shaped table. Two empty chairs were twisted outward. Two were occupied by Spelon and Tenor, who were also quietly conversing. I wondered briefly where the other guards had gone, the ones following at a distance. Had they departed yet, or were they standing outside, lined up like salt and pepper shakers at the doorway?

The black plexiglass surfaces of the table and chairs displayed reflections cast from various light spheres in the room. They partly livened up the effect of white on white — floors, ceilings, and walls all shiny and colorless. A Westlan residence had no windows in the front. What would there have been to see? No trees or plants, except in designated parks. No mountains, lakes, or landoors, the horse-like animals of Freinana. Everything was artificial on Westla, a planet whose outer frame was entirely made of metal.

Over to the left sat a food machine and a drink machine. Beside them stood the oval recycling bin. Behind me was an open doorway, which, if this were like Shaarvan's quarters, would lead to an entertainment room that held soft white carpet and fuzzy pillows. Probably on its white walls hung a tapestry or two. Most tapestries showed the Saberey, the Shapechanger emblem and symbol of their animal of Change. A few might host, instead, the Somber tree. A few displayed forests. Those were my favorite.

In the other direction would lie the bedrooms. Simplistic, unimaginative, and unvaried. The Shapechanger of Westla disliked objects that served no purpose and anything purely decorative or ornate.

A new thought struck me like a rock in a rolling barrel. It clanged against the sides, echoing in my head, calling me *Fool, fool, fool.* How could I have forgotten my sweet little son? He was still in the nursery. Would Stegthal permit my son's presence? My Second didn't seem like the type who would care for children. Spelon had told me once that Stegthal spent all his time studying. A baby was never quiet. What would I do if Stegthal refused to allow Shaarac to live with me in these quarters?

Stegthal, still in the middle of his discussion with Thedar, walked over to the table and sat in the chair beside me.

I dropped my eyes, but I reached out and caught at his sleeve. I risked much in disturbing him, but I had to know. "Please, Stegthal," I said, using my softest, most submissive voice. "Please, may Shaarac live here? Please, will you at least grant me that?"

The icy gray of stone in Stegthal's eyes softened. A hint of a smile made the gray of his eyes sparkle a moment before he nodded. "You can be very charming when you choose to, Shaara."

My back stiffened, but I breathed in deeply and kept my eyes lowered.

I could feel all their eyes watching me. I played their game and didn't look up.

After a moment, Stegthal chuckled. "Good. I am pleased that you have begun to think."

Again, his words stung, but I didn't react. I could ignore anything until he gave me a reply.

"Shaarac will, of course, live with us. I shall be taking care of both of you, my dear, just as Shaarvan requested."

I sighed, smiled, and glanced up. Something in his expression took my smile away. I breathed in sharply and lowered my eyes. I didn't want to think about the flash of desire I'd seen in his eyes.

But . . . " I started to state the obvious that Shaarac was still at the preschool.

Stegthal cut me off. He turned towards the others. "You will leave us now. Do not bring the baby until the quarter moon. My wife and I need time alone to discuss some things first."

One by one, my bondmates backed away, bid Stegthal and me a good Tide, and turned and left. I didn't look up as they retreated, nor speak. I couldn't forgive them for taking Stegthal's side.

When the last of them, Spelon, with his brow bulging darkly and his lips in position to speak, yet not doing so, had removed themselves from Stegthal's residence, my new Shapechanger Lord picked up my left hand and turned it palm upward. Instinctively, I attempted to pull back. Stegthal's eyes, the color of the dulled side of a shaded boulder, clamped into my soul. I resented the invasion, but he was inside me for only an instant, then freed me without a wave of his hand or a blink of an eye. I swallowed hard and stared at my vibrating knees.

Stegthal still held my hand, but as the seconds ticked, and he did nothing more, my knees stilled, and my heart stopped its horse race. He'd told the others we needed to talk, but I didn't want to hear anything he had to say. Yet the continued silence was almost as harsh.

I didn't want to look at him, either. My eyes searched the room. Somehow, I'd missed seeing a small Shapechanger plaque. It was not Altarian, not like the one Shaarvan had with forest greens and rich, dark browns. Stegthal's plaque was lavender, and the symbols were strange and unreadable. It held threads of wheat-gold and lime.

Stegthal's eyes followed mine. "Good," he said. "Study it well, my dear. On my planet, a wife has it freeze-branded right there, and her husband's coat of arms surrounds it."

Stegthal had reached over and placed his hand on my arm between my wrist and elbow to show me. I flinched. His touch seemed almost as painful as a branding would be.

"I hate it when you touch me," I said.

He tightened his grip on my wrist until I wondered if he'd crush my bones to prove his point. I tried to get him to release me. He'd left white marks on my skin. I stared down at them, remembering the bruises my Freinanan owner had inflicted.

Stegthal's eyes followed mine. He reached over and began massaging the marks away. "You are an interesting child," he said.

I bristled at his insult. By Earth's standards, I was a full adult already, or close to it. And on Freinana, I was certainly old enough to be bought, sold, and gambled with. I was a mother, too. Wasn't that supposed to give me rights with the Shapechanger?

But Stegthal didn't seem to notice my irritation.

"You are full of contrasts. Wild as a newly captured bride, yet sophisticated in Shapechanger training. You are frightened into cowering one moment, then bursting with unwise bravery the next. You interest me. I believe that once you have adapted, we shall meld well."

"Meld?" I squeaked out.

He patted my arm. "It means 'to get along," he said, then stood and moved away.

That wasn't my definition of the word, but I'd only studied Altarian for little more than a Pass. I hadn't used it much on Freinana. There were many words I didn't know and many shades of meaning.

Stegthal returned with a blue-hued goblet full of liquid and two small shot glasses. He poured an equal portion of the cream-colored liquid into each. My eyes watched his hands. Only my training with Tessa heightened my concentration so I was aware when he added something to mine. He handed me the drink, and I shook my head. His eyes flared a moment's green, and then he smiled.

My tongue was dry. My tears had taken all the moisture from my mouth. My throat cried out for the beverage he'd poured.

Stegthal lifted his and sipped. The drink fizzled loudly, destroying the silence of the room. My eyes were drawn to the liquid in the other glass. I wanted it desperately. Surely it would be OK to take just one sip . . . but my hand made no move towards it.

Stegthal's eyes again nodded a tribute. "You have strength, my dear." He moved closer and stood so near my hair bristled at the currents of his Power.

He reached out to touch my face. I cringed. His other hand, the left one, dropped down on my shoulder. The weight of it was a warning. I didn't move my body from the chair, but I raised my chin upwards and glared.

His right hand again moved towards my face. My eyes considered the hugeness of his fingers. His hand was larger than Shaarvan's, the fingers long and wide. This time, I could not avoid his touch. Nor could I hold back the gasp that fled through my parted lips as his fingers, cold as the ice of metal, stroked me. I froze my body, stilling myself not to whimper like a beaten dog, not to cower from his touch, but my eyes told him my thoughts. Had I the Power, I would have killed him for touching me.

He laughed softly, and his hand dropped. Only then was I aware of the taste of blood in my mouth. I had bitten through my lip. The sting of it was far less than the touch of a male's hand where only my husband's should be.

My head was high — my chin in stubborn mode, as Shaarvan would have said, but Stegthal cupped it with his hand and raised it even higher. His index finger reached out for my lip and opened my mouth further so he could see what I'd done.

"Silly child," he scolded.

He reached over with his hand, lifted up his glass, and held it against my lip. The cold of it was like Stegthal's touch.

The drink still babbled away. Its fizz was growing louder.

"In your eyes, you battle me." Stegthal's voice was a water melody, smooth and beckoning. There was a smell emanating from him, not an unpleasant one. My mind fought to label it, to breathe more of it in. Something was wrong. I tried to pull away from the coldness of the glass, the siren voice, the scent, the intoxicating fragrance of him, but his hand still clasped my chin. His grip allowed no withdrawal.

"It will do you little good to fight me, Child," Stegthal warned me gently. "Have you forgotten your Shapechanger training so easily?"

The little bit of training I'd been allowed with Tessa had not made me strong enough that Stegthal could threaten me with training and fail to see a reaction. I shuddered, and he nodded, pleased. The gray of his eyes softened. His lips exposed bone-white teeth and a smile that was devastatingly handsome. I began to tremble.

"Poor child," he said, letting go of my chin so he could take my hand. He removed his other hand from my shoulder and pulled the chair closer so he could sit beside me. "I think you are much more frightened than you admit. Is your rebellion only an attempt to hide your fear?"

My eyes were drawn to the fingers of Stegthal's hand. His long, heavy fingers were stroking my palm. The Power of a Shapechanger's touch on the palm leaves no will to fight. I knew I couldn't resist Stegthal if he continued.

I jerked my hand and launched myself towards the door, an action of my legs, not my brain. Panic terrorized me.

Stegthal had only to reach out with his long arms as I rocketed by. His reflexes were so fast I barely saw him move, and yet once again, I was entrapped.

"Stop your battles," Stegthal said as he brought me close against his long, hard body. "Shaarvan commanded you to obey me. Have you forgotten?"

I froze, remembering. Of course, I would obey the will of my husband, but Shaarvan had told me nothing about Stegthal touching me or demanding I live in a dwelling with him. Shaarvan had only told me that the marriage with Stegthal was to assure I would be cared for *if* Shaarvan were to die. Only then was I supposed to be Stegthal's.

I started to argue, but he flashed the silence command. Then, he pulled me down into his lap. I would have fought him over that, but he said, "I am Shapechanger — obey me."

No female who's gone through training can ever disobey that command. I stilled my body and sat as stiffly as possible, but I didn't resist when he jerked me back against his chest.

"You will listen now," he said, in the quiet, commanding voice of a Shapechanger Lord who offers no choice in the matter.

I bowed my head in submission, but he was still not appeased. "I have been patient long enough with your outbursts and your defiance."

An angry Shapechanger Lord is a dangerous male. The stiffness of my body quickly leaked away.

"Stars, Child! You are more volatile than an isotope missing an electron."

I didn't understand his words, but his hand was on my neck, and I remembered the strength in his fingers. I feared that this time, my spine would be pulverized if I dared move.

"I shall not hurt you. Stop your shivering, little one," Stegthal ordered with the same quiet voice.

But my body didn't listen. It trembled even more violently. I whimpered, hardly aware I'd done so.

The fingers on my neck released, and Stegthal's hands and arms scooped me up to place me back into a chair. Then he sat down beside me.

"Do not be frightened. I have told you I shall not hurt you." His eyes stared into mine — gray as night clouds, gray as the storm, then green, the diamonded green of the Shapechanger.

I felt his hands on my shoulder, pressing me down, although I do not remember attempting to get up. The glass was placed at my lips. Was it his glass or mine? I wanted to ask, but Stegthal was ordering me to drink, and my mouth was opening to obey. The liquid was bitter. I tried to turn away, but Stegthal's voice kept commanding me to drink. I swallowed.

I knew both from the taste and from my prior sight that the liquid was drugged, but my lips were obeying Stegthal's voice, and my mind couldn't overrule it. *Tessa*, I think I cried out, but there was no answering strength. The glass was half-emptied when Stegthal placed it down on the table.

"I am sorry, Child. I did not like the forcing of you. It is not the Shapechanger way, but neither would I have preferred to handle you with more roughness, and there seemed to be no other alternative."

His lips were at my ear, yet I heard him as if from a great distance. I turned my head. His eyes were watching me — owl eyes, huge and wise, yet gray once more.

Again, his hand reached out to caress the skin of my face. I could not cringe away from his fingers. I was frozen by his command and by the heat spreading through my body that urged me to lean into his touch. Stegthal's fingers grew as warm as the lethargy within me. My lips parted. Only the pain of moving my bitten lip tore me from Stegthal's trance. I pulled away.

He chuckled softly. "You are incredible, little one. So strong, so resilient. Your defiance should make me angry, but I find that it entices. I have rarely been so fascinated. Is it due to your changeability or to your childish rebellions? Perhaps a challenge is a good way for us to begin. I shall give you time, Child. Time to recover, to adapt, and to recognize your need."

His words were in the air all around me. I struggled to make sense of them, but a fog had descended, draping me in a kind of stupor. My arms felt limp, tired, and useless. Stegthal's lips were touching my ear, whispering and teasing.

"Shaarvan!" I whispered through my exhaustion. "What have you done?"

"He has saved your life, Child," Stegthal answered me and continued to stroke my face.

Why did I find myself craving a stranger's touch? What was he doing to me?

"Without me, my little wife, Thenos would kill you as easily as a hand crushes paper. I shall keep you safe. Do you not understand that, my little one?"

Shaarvan had gone to Altar to fight Thenos. How could Thenos injure me here?

My mouth was too dry to argue. "I do not feel well," I mumbled instead.

"The drug will not harm you. It only quiets your nerves so you can listen."

"I am too tired to listen. I need to sleep." I lay my head down on the table. The coolness of the plastic seemed welcome against the heat of my face. My eyes closed.

Stegthal bent over me and began to whisper into my ears. His lips so near my neck made me feel dizzy.

"Listen to me," he said. "You will understand about Second bonding and why you are here with me."

"I do understand. I will obey until Shaarvan comes." I forced out the words and then sighed sleepily.

"Yes, Child, but there is more. I am your husband, and you are mine in all ways until Shaarvan returns."

"Shaarvan," I repeated sleepily and smiled.

I think I fell asleep. I sensed Stegthal lifting me, but I couldn't open my eyes. They felt glued shut.

The arms that held me were strong and vaguely familiar. I listened to the rhythm of Stegthal's steady beating heart and felt safe inside his arms. I could feel the motion of his walk, so similar to Shaarvan's.

The same masculine thrust of the hips urged us forward. Like Shaarvan, Stegthal stepped lightly, a hunting cat, alert and agile.

"Ah, my lovely wife, I understand now why Shaarvan could not tell you." Stegthal's lips touched my forehead. I didn't fight. I was thinking how beautiful the word "Shaarvan" sounded on Stegthal's lips.

"Your mind holds your love for Shaarvan like a shield," Stegthal said.

I moved my head higher, closer to his heart. I liked the sound of Stegthal's heartbeat. It was almost like Shaarvan's.

In the bedroom, Stegthal pulled the covers back and then placed me on the bed. He covered me with a thick quilt and tucked in the sides. It was just like Shaarvan would have done it. Again, I smiled.

Once more, Stegthal's lips touched my brow. "Sleep, little one. Sleep."

I didn't listen to the quiet tread of his feet as he walked away. I was already dreaming of Shaarvan, the Shapechanger who would forever hold my heart.

Chapter Two

Spelon, on the artificial planet, Westla

We left when we were practically ordered out. I didn't like leaving. This is all wrong. Shaarvan never should have left her. No wife should be without her husband, no husband without his wife. That is the law on my planet, Despega, but apparently not on Shaarvan's.

Could views of marriage be that different? Could the needs of their women be so insignificant? Shaarvan not only leaves her behind with another, but he travels across the galaxy to his home. I would not do that. If Shaara were mine, I would never leave her.

And to wed her to another? What foolishness is this? Oh, I know it is done among the Warlords of other worlds, but I have seen it go sour more times than it has worked. A wife cannot be torn between two males. A woman is too soft to give allegiance to several, and so she chooses one of them as her preference. Even those Warlords who start as friends end as enemies when the woman comes between them.

It was not wise of Shaarvan, and I told him so, but his eyes told me the decision had been made. He heard me out, but he did not heed me. I informed him also that I did not agree with his choice for Second, and he warned me not to interfere — my good friend, warning me!

But I repeat it again. This Warlord that Shaarvan has left his wife with, I do not trust him. He hides something from us. Tenor or Thedar would have better served as guardian to the woman. And I, of course, would have given Shaarvan both steadfastness and honor. But this Stegthal wears a wall against us, even when issues of importance are not in discussion. What does he hide? How does Shaarvan know Stegthal can be trusted with the boy and with his wife?

I shall watch the Warlord like an eagle, like the Soaring Eagle who circles on high with eyes far-seeing as the Old Ones. And, if I do not like what I see, I shall seize her from his grasp. Tenor and Thedar will both back me. They, too, are uneasy as to Stegthal's governing of Shaarvan's woman.

No, that is not true. With all honesty, I cannot affirm that. Tenor will not lightly cede the woman to me. His eyes did not hold the certainty of mine. He may prove troublesome. What was it he said?

I remember. I recall his discourse. Tenor argued that Stegthal was Shaarvan's choice and thus irrevocable. Yet Tenor did agree our protection of Shaara required us to keep a close watch on Stegthal.

Then Thedar spoke. "If we were forced to take the girl away from Stegthal, I wonder what harm it would do her? She rebels against the Warlord, as she would against any of us. We must be a united front. We cannot do otherwise. And, besides, did you notice how she clung to Stegthal's shirt after Shaarvan's ship went through the eye?"

As if a hysterical woman had any knowledge of her actions! Of course, I negated Thedar's words, but I was overrun with their denials. They had already heard several times how I thought Shaarvan's wife needed a stronger hand.

"Even a Somber Tree cannot grow tall in shifting sand."

"What in the Stars does that mean, Tenor?" I demanded.

"The girl is our charge . . ." Tenor began.

"Would you two stop calling her a girl!" I stormed. "Shaara is small, but her body is appropriate to her age and size, and she has borne Shaarvan a son."

"I am aware of that, Spelon," Tenor said, smiling in the slightly superior manner he gets at times. "I am aware of all of Shaara's history. Are you? Let me remind you. Her parents passed on early. Then, she had only an old woman to care for her. That woman also passed. And then Shaara was taken captive by Shaarvan, only to be seized again and sold as a slave. No sooner does she adapt to that than Shaarvan grabs her again. And now, she is left with a stranger.

"The child . . ." Tenor stopped and looked up at me as if to see if I would interrupt again, but I had been thinking about what he said. When he put it like that, it was easy to understand why Shaara seemed so young. Females were adaptable. Everyone knew that, but Shaara had been through more than most. And she was very young still. Most girls her age had not yet even been seeded.

Tenor continued, and I had to force my thoughts to catch up.

"Since she has had so little stability in her life, it increases the risk of her ending up like Temina."

I interrupted him. "Shaarvan's wife is nothing like Temina. Shaara is quick and bright. She . . ."

Thedar stopped me with his hand on my arm. "They are from the same planet, Spelon. And Tem continually insists that Temina is intelligent. I am not saying that Shaara would . . ."

"What are you saying?" I demanded, shaking off Thedar's hand.

"Only this. If we want to keep the girl sound, it would be better if we not uproot what Shaarvan has so carefully planned."

My two friends gave sensible arguments. I did not like Shaarvan's decision, but I would leave it until Stegthal showed his true character. If Stegthal hurt her, I would kill him. Until then, I would lie in wait. But Shaara should have been mine.

Tren, onboard a spaceship bound for Westla

Had anyone told me that I, a mere Commoner, would be accompanying a Shapechanger back to Westla, I would not have believed him. It was said that no one, except those of the Shapechanger breed, had ever been allowed to land on the artificial satellite of the Shapechanger. I was still reeling from the shock of Shaarvan's invitation.

Targone was accompanying me, which was good, but still the trip to Westla was not exactly comfortable. I suppose it is never easy traveling with those of a different species. The fact that each of them, down to the lowest of the ship's guards, was more powerful than I, was a tough grain to chew.

The captain, Jorvanel, spent a great deal of his time telling me stories of the Shapechanger. I think I heard all the Legends and most of the Chants during those times of sharing. I appreciated the education until Targone urged me to memorize the Chants. I was not sure how wise that was. Were not the Shapechanger usually more secretive than Jorvanel and Targone led me to believe? How much would they permit me to know before their guard went up, and they regretted my knowledge?

I reminded Targone often that I had made no decision yet. It was a great honor to be offered to become a Shapechanger, but I did not know if I wanted my body altered. What would that be like? Hadn't I always been content with the man I was?

I could tell Targone thought my hesitation ludicrous. Shaarvan's proposal was a package deal — position, family, money, and a chance to become a member of what I think Targone viewed as a super race.

But I needed time to make the decision. I wanted to see what Westla was like, to have the opportunity to meet others of the race, to see if it was truly worth a stretch of time in deep sleep in some nebulous transition period that Targone seemed unwilling to discuss.

Yet, on the other side of the proposition was the fact that only as a Shapechanger could I see Shaara again. What would it be like to be her brother? Would it be enough? Was it worth Transition?

Shaara, on the artificial planet, Westla

When I woke, it was morning, and the memory of Shaarvan's ship disappearing like a reversed shooting star brought tears to my eyes. I was just about to have that private little session of crying I'd promised myself when my eyes landed on the pillow next to mine. A heavy head had left an indentation in the pillow's plumpness, and a short black hair that was definitely not mine lay in the valley. The coverings of the bed had been thrown back carelessly on that side, too. It was obvious I hadn't been alone through the night.

I rose and glanced around the chamber. My dress from the Tide before lay on the ground. I had no memory of removing it. My heart beat faster as my anger grew.

The room was extremely sparse in its decor. Only a bed and an empty chair occupied the room. The chair was of the same make as the eating room's furniture — black plastic-glass — and the bed was the usual wooden -mounted shush with its hard, body-adapting liquid.

The carpeting was white and soft enough that I could still walk on it despite a blistered heal. I hobbled over to the necessary room. When I was clean and dry, and my blister popped and treated by the antiseptic water unit, I began to search for the clothes that Stegthal should have placed out for me — he had left me nothing.

I dressed myself in the used lavender gown of the Tide before. The material luckily did not wrinkle, but Shapechanger are meticulous in their cleanliness. No garment was ever worn twice.

The dress was also unsuitable. It was a Westlan ceremonial gown and required the assistance of one's husband. The buttons up the back were impossible for me to completely fasten. By skewering the dress around, I managed all except the eight top ones. It was not only irritatingly difficult, but I kept remembering the feel of Shaarvan's warm fingers stroking my skin as he'd buttoned me the Tide before. How could I endure Shaarvan's absence? How long would he be gone?

I found my son, Shaarac, in a little bed in the room next to where I'd slept. His black eyelashes fluttered only a moment as I bent over to kiss his cheek. As usual, he was sucking away at his pointer finger. I pulled it loose. The finger was red and swollen, rough textured from its nightly battle with Shaarac's sucking mouth. Immediately, the baby began to fret. For a moment, I feared I'd awakened him, but

Shaarac turned over, and the finger disappeared. Once more, my son was happily sucking away. I slipped out quietly.

It was difficult to remember the cold hardness of my anger as I left Shaarac. The sight of him as always softened me, churning my insides with feelings that left me weak with love. I leaned my head against a wall, savoring its coolness on my cheek.

As I stood there, my eyes scanned the parts of the dwelling I hadn't seen. The plainness of everything seemed almost jarring to me. I had grown used to the wealth of Shaarvan's position. The tapestries, the plantings, and the flowered carpeting were all missing in Stegthal's chambers. The starkness was depressing.

I forced myself to search for the strange bondmate who was now responsible for Shaarac and me. I found him sitting at his computer in a small chamber he had turned into an office. He was peering at the smallest monitor screen I'd ever seen since leaving my native planet. His eyes were focused on strange mathematical symbols that ran across the screen, filling it in all directions.

He was mumbling words in a non-Altarian tongue, like a chant in highs and lows. Had the room been draped in spider webs and hanging bats, I would have labeled Stegthal a sorcerer working on magic incantations.

All about him on the floor were scatterings of papers and old-fashioned leather-bound books in heaps and piles. To the right of him, a table was filled with more papers, books, and metal objects that had wires of copper and brass poking outward at odd angles. I wanted to examine everything and ask a hundred questions, but there were things more important than curiosity.

Quietly, I reached out for one of the softbound books lying on the table. It fit in my hand perfectly. I pulled back my arm, aimed for Stegthal's back, and launched my missile.

Perhaps Stegthal had heard my approach, although I'd made no noise, but Shapechanger have cat-like hearing. Without turning his head or body, Stegthal's hand flew up, and he caught my flying missile neatly in his palm. He reached over, placed the book down by his chair, and then twisted around to stare at me. The look in his eyes made the words I had prepared clog thickly in my throat.

I caught myself before I'd taken more than two steps backward. I raised up my chin and spat out my words. "You have betrayed Shaarvan. You drugged me, and then you slept in the same bed with me. How can you call yourself Shaarvan's friend? You are a traitor and a . . ."

I was well-familiar with the agility of the Shapechanger male, but even so, the speed of Stegthal's spring surprised me. I had not even finished my accusations before his hand seized my shoulder, and he was dragging me towards him. A whimper of fear erupted before I could clamp my mouth shut.

There was only one section of the wall devoid of the leaning towers of books and papers. Stegthal pushed my back up against it. He didn't hurt me, but the coldness I thought I saw in his eyes was frightening. I wished that Stegthal would yell or curse at me or even strike me and get it over with, but he just stood there, staring at me like I was an amoeba he'd decided to study.

His hand moved upwards, and I was sure for some reason that he'd decided to strangle me. Like a Tide-old helium balloon, I sagged downwards. Stegthal's hands lifted me back.

"Be still," Stegthal ordered. His hand lifted up. I thought he meant to hit me, so I shut my eyes, tucked my chin, and waited for the blow. My eyes pressed shut so tightly that I saw the most beautiful golden circles before they faded away into darkness. Yet, no fist shot out. No pain lanced my cheek.

"Easy child. I have no intention of hitting you."

I felt Stegthal's hand slow its movement. The touch of his fingers breathed a whisper on my cheek. Then, his hand was brushing back my hair and playing with a lock of it, and the same quiet voice continued a soothing melody of gentle tones.

Why did I tremble more? I opened my eyes cautiously.

His hand moved slowly down to touch my chin. He cupped it and raised my head. "You are my wife, Shaara. I do not wish to hurt you, but you *must* listen."

He was Shapechanger, but he didn't act like Shapechanger. It puzzled me.

"I tried to tell you last night while you were drugged. Even then, I could not make you absorb the information."

He spoke in a tone barely louder than a whisper. I held my breath to hear him.

His face and his body were too close. His warm breath in my ear was frightening. The thumping of my heart sounded like a drum roll. I shivered.

His body stiffened away from me, and he loosened the hold on my eyes. I breathed in great gulps of air, relieved to be free of his Shapechanger magic and the feel of his body pressing against mine.

Had we not struggled? The towers of papers at my right still perched at an awkward angle, looking undisturbed. The books beside it climbed each other's backs and lay there passively.

Stegthal had released me. Could I bolt to the door?

As if I'd voiced the thought aloud, two hands were once again on my shoulders, and his eyes bored into mine.

"Enough," Stegthal said, tightening his grip until I winced. "Stop it, girl. You *will listen* to me now."

"I am not a *girl!*" I said. It was breaking training to raise my voice to a male, but Stegthal kept insulting me.

A Shapechanger female earns her title of *woman* when she bears her first child. The pain of childbirth pulls her into full Shapechanger by completing the chromosome metamorphosis in her body. It is not an easy Change, and for some the alienness of it strains the mind to breaking. But a girl who travels through the Change completely is no longer *a girl*. She is a Shapechanger woman. I had earned that right. No male could take it from me.

And as if to prove my case, Shaarac awakened then, and his screams at finding himself in a strange room pierced the battle zone between Stegthal and myself.

"This is not finished, child-woman," Stegthal warned me. His eyes burned into mine, and then abruptly, he dropped his hands from my shoulders and turned towards the door.

I followed, scarcely breathing. Had my voice been too loud? Had I yelled? It was a grave crime where males were concerned.

I called out to Shaarac that I was coming, but Stegthal still barred my way. His eyes stared down at me. At first I didn't move, not even to lower my eyes in the manner I'd been trained. But then I glanced over in the direction of Shaarac's room. Perhaps hearing my voice had soothed him. His cries had mellowed into fretting.

"I have called you *girl,* not meaning it as an insult to your Shapechanger status," Stegthal said calmly. "It is merely that you are a child in your storms of temperament."

He paused a moment as if checking to see if I was listening. "I do not believe that bearing your husband an heir should render you into adulthood, my dear.

"Adulthood is earned by demonstrating wisdom. Wisdom, patience, and temperance."

Each word lashed at me viciously. They were a pile of insults, but my eyes grew misty with moisture. I gritted my teeth, trying to stop the fall of fresh tears sliding down my cheeks.

For a moment, neither of us spoke. I didn't have the control. Perhaps Stegthal had nothing more to say.

I could hear Shaarac's fussing in the other room. It was rising in volume. Another minute and his wails would become a full-voiced, red-faced scream of anger.

"Please, may I go to him?" I asked, my head lowered, my voice carefully modulated.

"Perhaps I do see the beginnings of intelligence in your emotionally bloated brain," Stegthal said.

I gasped. Stars! Why was he such a jerk? Immediately, my tears were done. I wished I had another book to throw.

Stegthal's smile flickered out. His eyes grew stern again. "First lesson, Shaara. There is a fine line between bravery and foolishness. You are very near the edge, my dear. Careful."

The way he said *careful* pricked my skin. It was almost as if Stegthal held a dagger at my throat and pressed inward slowly, his eyes not only assessing the amount of blood that flowed in my veins but analyzing the necessary depth to push. His delivery was that coldly calculated. The air left my lungs as Stegthal continued to watch me with his cobra's eyes.

When he finally allowed me to pass, I bolted through the doorway. Despite Shaarac's escalating cries, it took me another moment before I could enter my son's room. The trembling in my body and the fear that poured throughout my system were not seemly in the mother of Shaarvan's son. I called forth my training with Tessa. My fear curled into a little ball. Calming breaths and the cold wall I leaned on bolstered me until I was ready.

My son was soaking wet. Whoever had put him down the night before had not checked his potty pants first. Shaarac didn't seem to care. His arms and legs wiggled energetically as he laughed at my efforts to remove the soiled diaper. I kissed him and carried him to the necessary. In a minute, the dry shower had him smelling sweet. But I couldn't clothe him in fresh clothes. I didn't know how to operate the clothes machine.

For a few moments, I played peekaboo with my son. I loved to hear his laughter, and his smile was just like Shaarvan's. But I could put it off no longer. I pushed hard at the little ball of fear wedged down inside me. I kissed my son, then picked him up, and carried him nude as a Tenlop into Stegthal's office.

At the doorway, the sight of Stegthal turning around to look at me almost made me lose my courage. I stood there gulping in air, and the words wouldn't come. The baby was giggling and squirming, wanting to be free to crawl about. Stegthal rose and walked towards me. He reached out and took Shaarac, and still I was mute.

"Why have you not clothed the boy?" Stegthal's voice came out in a normal tone as if my earlier confrontation had not occurred. Yet his eyes brushed me with coldness, and shivers played tag up and down my back. Stegthal smiled at Shaarac and began lifting him up and down in the air. Shaarac laughed. Already, my son seemed comfortable with the giant Shapechanger.

Once again, Stegthal's eyes focused on me, eyes of a winter wind that seeps down through the thickest coverings. I shivered, feeling the fingers of ice touching my skin. I struggled to answer, but my voice had fled.

"Speak up, girl. You have demonstrated your ability to do so when you wish."

Was it another warning? I didn't think he'd punish me in front of Shaarac, but I forced myself to tell him my problem.

Stegthal had resumed his play with Shaarac, but his eyes flooded me with his attention. "Shaarvan never taught you to program?"

I shook my head and stared at the floor. Would Stegthal make me feel as stupid as Shaarvan had at first? My native planet was backward compared to the technologies of Altar and Westla.

Shaarac became quiet as if he, too, were thinking over the problem. I looked up. He was sucking his finger, absorbed in studying Stegthal's face.

At that moment, I felt a gentle touch of Stegthal's mind inside my head. Like a feather duster flicking across my arm, Stegthal's touch was there no more than a second and then gone.

The War Lord moved closer. His hand reached out to stroke my throat, a Shapechanger command to look up.

"Ignorant, possibly," Stegthal said. "Stupid, no. And of the two, Shaara, I much prefer ignorance. It is far easier to correct.

Come, girl," he said, waving Shaarac's arm as if the baby were giving directions. For a moment, I almost smiled.

As we walked to Shaarac's room, I listened to Shaarac's happy cooing. It was as if he'd already been fed his bottle. How could a stranger find favor so easily in my son's eyes?

Following the directions given, I pressed my hand against the machine's receptor to imprint my touch. Next, Stegthal showed me how to program for the item desired.

I followed the sequence, but Shaarac's first rompers came out in lavender. Stegthal was busy playing with Shaarac, so I programmed it again. But the machine refused to issue the proper Altarian green. My mistakes accumulated four clear packages of insipid pale lavender.

"I must be doing something wrong," I said. "I can't get it to issue the right color."

Stegthal listened, then smiled a flash of teeth. "The color of the garment is your only problem?" Without waiting, he was already handing back my son. "I have keyed in the lavender," he said. "You and Shaarac will wear no other color."

Stegthal reached over and patted Shaarac's head before continuing. "Since you are obviously proficient in your programming now," he said, his eyes viewing my pile on the floor, "I shall return to my work."

Stegthal was already retreating back into his office when the full meaning hit me. I dressed Shaarac in the lavender romper, took time to feed him the bottle Stegthal had brought me, and then I went barging in after Stegthal.

"I hate lavender," I told Stegthal. "And Altarians wear green, forest green."

Stegthal was standing by his table when I interrupted. He turned and looked back at me. "You are bold, but are you wise?"

I shifted Shaarac to my other side. He was growing faster than a Terran child and was heavy. "I am wise enough to know what color Shaarac and I should be wearing," I replied cautiously.

"Good. Then, you will be content that the machines are set to lavender. You and Shaarac are under *my* protection, and so you both wear *my* color."

Stegthal flashed the *no argument sign,* and then his hand behind my back propelled me to the eating room. There, he showed me how to program food, including Shaarac's bottles.

The rest of the Tide continued in the same vein. A war was waging that Stegthal and I would not fight in front of Shaarac, but every word ruffled the borders between us. All that morning, I shot glares of hatred that would have wounded a lesser male. Stegthal's eyes took on the speckled green of an angry Shapechanger.

My bondmates arrived in the afternoon. I was so delighted to see them I forgot my anger. I would have rushed into their arms for bear hugs, but Stegthal chose that moment to take his revenge.

"Sit in the chair, girl, and do not move," he ordered abruptly.

I followed Stegthal's finger to the kitchen chair and plopped down angrily. My eyes glowered.

Thedar came over and removed the baby from my arms. Instead of being understanding, Thedar shook his head at me. He carried Shaarac off into the central room, and the others followed. I couldn't see my son and my bondmates, but I could hear them playing with Shaarac, laughing comfortably.

In the quiet moments, when Shaarac's giggles subsided enough for me to hear their voices, I strained my ears, attempting to hear if they spoke of Shaarvan.

For a long time, I sat on the chair, scowling at the wall. I made one quiet dash to the door just to double check it was still locked. The electric field on it wiggled the hairs on my hand. I knew not to touch the door. I was returning to my prison chair when Stegthal's voice rang out, "Do not leave the chair again." How had he known I'd moved?

My stomach growled. I'd skipped the morning meal, my appetite nonexistent, but sitting with nothing to do added hunger to my list of grievances.

It seemed as if the punishment would go on forever. My stomach growled, my throat felt parched, and I was bored and brimming with anger. And I hated being ignored.

Finally, Spelon came in and joined me. He sat, choosing the chair furthest away. Did he think disobedience was contagious?

"Are you all right, Shaara?" he asked.

"No. How could I be all right? Shaarvan has left me here with this . . . this . . . " I couldn't think of anything bad enough to call Stegthal.

Most of my swear words were Freinanan, and being called a *spithead* wasn't much of an insult to a Shapechanger.

"Careful," Spelon warned. I could tell from his nervousness that the image I'd visualized had given him the idea. "Whatever the reason for your anger, Stegthal is a Shapechanger Lord. Respect that."

It was wise not to rile Spelon, too. Already, his high cheekbones were rigid with affront. Even the close-clipped hairs of his soldier cut seemed to bristle.

I looked down, attempting to appease him, but he wasn't placated.

"Tenor, Thedar, and I know little of Stegthal. He was Shaarvan's friend, not ours, but my instincts as a Warrior tell me he is dangerously unpredictable. Look at me, Shaara."

I raised my eyes obediently. I hoped Spelon could not read me as cleverly as Stegthal could. If Spelon did, this lecture would continue all night.

"Little bondmate, your strength is nothing to us," he said, shaking his head. "You are merely a captured female. Why do you resist? Stegthal will give you much pain."

Worry was painting Spelon's sky-gray eyes a smudgy dark. It surprised me that he cared.

"Stegthal slept with me last night, Spelon. Won't Shaarvan kill him for that?"

Spelon's face looked puzzled. "Stegthal is your husband, Shaara. Shaarvan gave you to him. Why should he be angry because Stegthal beds you?"

Had the world gone crazy? Shaarvan wouldn't . . .

The sound of my chair hitting the flooring woke me to the fact that I was standing up. I was also screaming at Spelon, "You're a liar, you're a liar," over and over.

A quiet voice from behind me pierced my litany. "Go to your room, girl," he said.

I was already moving, but as I passed him, I looked up. Stegthal's eyes had Changed into the tiger-eyes that Shapechanger bore when intensely angry. I had once felt the claws of an enraged Shapechanger. They had torn long, deep gouges into the skin of my arms.

I flashed the sign of submission and rushed past him. Thedar and Tenor stood near the doorway of the entertainment room. Neither of them spoke to me.

Shaarac cried out. I wheeled about and raised my hands to take him.

"No. Shaarac stays with us," Stegthal said.

Behind me, I heard my son already beginning to laugh. His fears were so easily soothed. He was too young to be hurt if someone said that his father had given us away.

Could what Spelon have said be true? Had Shaarvan really given me to Stegthal? Did Shaarvan no longer want me?

I sat in the chair across from the bed where I'd slept. In our absence, the Bed Machine had straightened and smoothed it. What would happen tonight? Did I belong to Stegthal in the same way I'd belonged to Shaarvan?

I sat still so long the room's artificial light darkened, and still I didn't move. I had no more tears left, no more wild ideas, no plans for the future. I hurt all over. I thought maybe I was ill. Was it possible to die from a heart ripped into shreds?

If I were dead, Shaarvan and my bondmates would not need to worry about my welfare. Shaarac wouldn't be alone. He would have the bondmates. My son had already forgotten me. He was probably laughing in the other room, content to be with the males. In many ways, he was exactly like his father. Perhaps Shaarac had abandoned me, too.

At last, the outer door opened and closed, and then there was a stillness that told me the Shapechanger had taken Shaarac. I prayed Stegthal had gone, too, but Shapechanger code forbade leaving a woman alone.

I heard footsteps approaching the door. I looked for a place to hide, knowing, even as I did so, that I wouldn't move. The door slid open. I didn't look up. My eyes were riveted to the floor. The swirling patterns made me feel dizzy, but anything was better than seeing the anger in Stegthal's Shapechanger eyes.

"Come here," Stegthal ordered.

My eyes fluttered upward, but my feet were already moving. I went towards him slowly, draggingly, and stopped about a foot away. It was then that it hit me. I had no idea what this Shapechanger would do to me. Before, I'd only considered Stegthal a kind of babysitter for Shaarvan, but if what Spelon said was true . . .

Stegthal reached out with his giant hands and pulled me close. I felt limp of direction and body-frozen. Arms encircled me, almost tucking me into the male's massive body. My head, crushed against his chest, oddly found comfort in the sound of his heartbeat, the soft persistence of it, the continuity.

Without conscious thought, my tears started once more, and I was crying into Stegthal's shirt, clinging like a child to its parent. Stegthal's hands patted me, massaging my back until the tears slowed and I calmed. Then, he led me to the bed and pushed me down gently beside him.

"I am sorry that it hurts so. I tried to explain last night and again this morning, but you were not ready. Perhaps Spelon did it more gently than I could have."

"He wasn't gentle. But what does it matter? Shaarvan has left me, and I want to die."

Stegthal's hand stopped caressing. "Stop that, Child. Shaarvan will come back for you. This is not forever. He told you that, did he not?"

"If Shaarvan loved me, he'd never have left me. Why don't you just tell me the truth?"

"Look at me," Stegthal demanded sharply. "I am Shapechanger. Know me. I do not lie. We are bonded, you and I. Do you not feel the truth in me?"

I searched the face of the bondmate I knew the least. His hair, straight and so dark it seemed black, had fallen forward into his eyes. The strands covered his dark, thick eyelashes on one side. My fingers lifted to smooth it back, then drifted down to the sharp bones of his arched cheek. Under my touch, the granite hardness softened. Why was I seeing Stegthal so differently? Why did I yearn to touch my lips to his?

I blinked my eyes, fighting the pull. Shapechanger magic, of course.

His eyes coaxed. His lips drew me. But there was no golden glint in his hair. No laugh lines around his eyes. His eyes called, but they weren't Shaarvan's eyes. I couldn't do this. Didn't he understand?

"Yes, I understand," he said, then sighed. "You resist me still. Little Shaara, what strength you have for a female and for one so young!" Stegthal smiled a sad smile, cupped my chin, and raised it so he could watch my eyes. "Calm yourself," he ordered. "I shall not rush you. We shall talk — nothing else."

I drew in breath, finding, suddenly, that my body felt starved for air. Stegthal waited a moment, then moved me to the bed to sit.

"Shaarvan did not want to leave you, Shaara. He could not take you with him. You project almost continuously — every thought, every emotion. Did you not know that?"

I nodded.

Stegthal's eyes poured into me, the gray of twilight, of skies stretching upwards endlessly. "Untrained as you are . . ."

I tried to interrupt to tell him about my training with Tessa, but his finger touched my lips in the silence command.

"You are still untrained, untrained to the point you would have drawn Thenos to you, no matter where you hid. That would have brought destruction down on the very Altarians Shaarvan went to protect."

I gasped. "How? How could I endanger anyone? Spelon says . . ." I stopped, realizing I'd spoken despite the silence command. My fingers flashed a quick sign of apology.

"Do you always fluctuate so wildly?"

I lowered my head.

"I am not angered, Shaara. I recognize the difference between confrontational and forgetful."

He raised my chin. "Spelon is wrong, Shaara. The potential of your Power is great, but it is the control that you need to work on."

We talked for a long while. Stegthal explained many things I had not understood. It was my stomach that ended our discussion. It began to grumble and gurgle in protest. Stegthal laughed and stood up, holding his hand out for me to accept. We were bonded and a certain freedom came with that, but placing my hand in Stegthal's that Tide implied more than it would have with the others. Although I did not know it then, it was the beginning of my acceptance of Stegthal's rights.

Thenos, in the Palace on Altar

The Shapechanger of Altar have formed an army against me. They think they can stop me. I laugh at their attempts. The palace is mine, as well as millions of dirtwalkers and the government. It is too late for the sleeping few to waken.

I have spies watching my mother and her Second, my brother Pathe, and all their friends. My suspicions are that they have joined forces against me. Yet, I have no proof, and they remain in their dwellings, seemingly innocent. I hope I am wrong. To kill my beautiful mother and my brother — this, I would not like to do. Yet, if the proof arrives, I shall order their deaths.

My spies have told me that Shaarvan has left Westla. I am relieved. In a Three-Tide, my wife will be sitting at my side. I have ordered more preparations for her arrival. Two serving slaves have been trained to provide for her needs. They will attend to her, and also inform me of her every waking moment.

I have installed five guards in the room beside hers, Commoners who have shown promise in weaponry. The serving slaves shall accompany my princess at all times. I have no fear the Commoner guards would dare to touch her, but there will be safeguards. And, of course, I shall lie by her side at night. When darkness falls, my wife will never be unattended.

My biggest worry will be the separation of Shaara from Shaarvan. I do not want my princess harmed. I have trained the men on my plan of attack. The moment Shaarvan lands and lowers his ramp, the same gas that disabled him before will once more do its service.

Then, the special Queen's guard will bring my princess to me. I dislike the idea of her being in a Commoner's arms, but it is almost certain that Shaarvan will land in a Shapechanger battle zone. I cannot enter there. It would be too dangerous.

No matter, I shall purge my princess' skin of the Commoner's touch. I have constructed a deep tank, which will be filled with scented water. I, myself, shall lower her into it. I shall enjoy the feel of her naked body in my arms as I soap the contamination away. Pity she will need to be unconscious. I should so like to see her eyes widen with her fear. Alas, it will not be long. I must be patient.

Shaara, on the artificial planet, Westla

Stegthal led me into the eating room, where I had spent most of the morning.

"We shall dine on the food machine's selections, my dear," he told me. "You will find it contains an exotic menu."

I had sampled many Shapechanger choices with Shaarvan. I wasn't fond of the unusual.

I stood, not knowing whether to sit down or to attempt to provide Stegthal with service. Shaarvan would have pointed to the chair where he wished me to sit, but on Freinana, I was the one who brought the food. My fingers wrapped nervously around the chair's back as I waited for directions, but Stegthal had turned away from me. His fingers were programming. He took no notice of my actions. He moved to the drink machine. A moment later, he turned. His hands held two rectangular biscuits.

"Do you not desire a seat?" he asked as he set the food down.

I sat in the closest chair, nervous in the awkwardness of my confusion. It had been so much easier when I hadn't cared if I pleased him.

"What is it?" I asked as I picked up one of the biscuits he handed me.

When he returned with our drinks, he sat beside me. "Florian dislo," he said, taking a bite of his.

My finger poked at it. It wasn't soft like the Altarian cakes Shaarvan had often given me. It was more like a dried-up piece of meat. The dull gray-brown of its outer surface was about as appealing as nibbling on tree bark. "Is it safe for me to eat?" I asked. "I think my body was only programmed for Altar and Freinana."

"We are both Shapechanger, remember? It does not matter from what planet. What I eat, you can always safely eat."

He saw me looking at the glass he had placed on the table in front of me and smiled, "Yes, the drink is untainted."

I sipped at it and found it similar to those I had drunk before. Without the bitterness of the drug Stegthal had added, I enjoyed its flavor.

I attempted to take a bite of the dislo. It didn't crumble as I expected, and my teeth couldn't pierce its surface. I watched Stegthal gnawing away on the edges of his. I scraped a layer of dislo. The taste was not objectionable. It reminded me of nuts and carrot cake, yet not sweet.

For a time, Stegthal didn't speak. His eyes seemed unfocused as he stared at the unadorned wall across from us.

I satisfied my hunger. Then, tired of gnawing at the hard, dry biscuit, I put the remains of it down on the table.

Stegthal's eyes were still frozen to the wall. He continued scraping at his dislo. I leaned forward onto my elbows and gave him the whole of my attention.

I supposed he was handsome in a way completely opposite of Shaarvan. Stegthal was dark — his hair, his eyes, even his skin, which had a slightly olive cast. He was big-boned like Shaarvan but not as light or as quick of foot. But there was no question of his might. His body was lean and strong. Even in his facial structure, the strength and power of his bones was evident. His jaws were moving rhythmically, but the motion made the angles of his face seem more masculine, more formidable.

His eyes met mine. "So now, we study each other. It is a way to become acquainted, I suppose, although I prefer touch." He reached out his hand to brush back a lock of my hair. I stilled myself not to cringe, and he chuckled softly.

"Your hair feels different than one expects. It is soft and has tiny springs of life that curl and weave among the strands. I have observed the way it falls at your back. The colors of it intertwine, as if nature were undecided in its hue, yet in its lack of choosing, chose excellently."

I fidgeted slightly, uneasy with such praise.

"Be still, Child," he ordered, smiling, then released the lock of hair. "Rarely am I intrigued long by things within my proximity," he said and continued on with his munching and scraping of the biscuit.

Stegthal seemed even harder than Shaarvan to figure out. Restlessly, I waited for him to finish eating. Dislo didn't seem to be a quick meal. My mind drifted back to my Tides on Freinana.

"Tell me about the landoors," Stegthal said, suddenly pulling me from my memories.

No Shapechanger male wastes time on trivia. The command surprised me by its nature as much as it challenged me with its difficulty. Providing information to Shapechanger had its own protocol — only the factual, nothing subjective.

I attempted to please him. "Landoors have fine heads — elongated and triangular. Their eyes are located at the broader section of the triangle. Their ears are rounded at the bottom but point upwards and are attached at the top of a landoor's head. The ears stretch up about a finger's length above the poll. A round snout of a nose and a mouth are located at the opposite end of the triangle."

Stegthal's eyes were closed. I halted, wondering if I'd put him to sleep.

"Go on," Stegthal said without opening his eyes.

I drew breath, and my words continued, but I was struggling with my thoughts. Why was Stegthal asking this? Was I being tested? What did he wish to hear?

"The body of the landoor is much larger than a Shapechanger male. The animal walks on four legs, having no other limbs. Therefore, it is without hands and fingers.

"Attached to one end of its body is a long, arched neck. The neck has a great deal of mobility. It allows the animal to touch the ground with its mouth. The landoor can also toss its neck slightly about from side to side, and it can push its head upward, higher than the rest of its body. Please, is that not enough?"

"Continue," Stegthal ordered. His eyes remained closed, the eyelashes, dark and long.

"But I don't know what else to say. What do you want to know?"

Stegthal opened his eyes to look at me. I could not begin to read his expression. The attention of his eyes confused me.

"Continue as you are, Child. Tell me everything about landoors that you know."

I closed my eyes to shut out his gaze and centered my thoughts. I was rambling, and I knew Stegthal would be displeased if I continued, but giving Shapechanger discourse was not my forte. Shaarvan had often been irritated by the senselessness of what he called my *emotional babble*. Would it anger Stegthal as well?

Facts, I kept whispering in my mind. Give him only that which is observable.

"Landoors have thin legs that end on hardened feet so they can carry weight on their backs and run long distances. Their legs are agile and can lift backward, folding up against their body for jumping over obstacles."

I stopped, afraid that I would begin to dwell on the delights of jumping and forget my Shapechanger objectivity. I scanned for something else to say.

"Landoors . . . landoors cannot talk using words, but through their eyes and ears, the carriage of their head, and the arching of their neck, they express emotions and desires. When you ride a landoor, you can feel those thoughts through the slight movements of their body and through the force inside them — a force almost like the feel of the current of a river as it brushes against your legs. This force ripples with the eagerness of the landoor's muscles whenever it lunges forward.

And, if you are connected with the landoor's thoughts and urges, the power in his stride and the speed at which he gallops across the ground at times drives you into a wild abandonment of thought. But, it is your control over this wildness that the landoor respects, and when your body sits up straighter and your back becomes more rigid, that is the curb that holds power over the landoor."

I stopped. There was so much more I could have said about the way landoors made me feel or the joy of riding them, but that was all subjective, and already my words reeked of emotion.

I dropped my head to stare at my hands. They were clenched as if they felt the softness of the leather reins between their fingers. I loosened them and attempted to relax. I found that I was short of breath as if I'd been astride Crimson Black, the landoor I'd loved on Freinana. I was as tired as if I'd just completed a heavy session of training on his back and perspiring in equal measure.

"Shaara," Stegthal said, and I looked up, surprised to hear my name on his lips. It had always been *Child* or *Girl*. "Shaarvan has trained you well," he said, nodding that he was pleased. Stegthal had formed a steeple with his fingers and was sliding them up and down soundlessly. I could almost feel the touch of his finger pads on my skin. I shivered and looked away.

"You invite my attention, child. There is a quality . . . a depth in you that is not at first evident. And under pressure, you seem more able to channel your emotions than I had supposed. With more training . . ."

He did not continue his thoughts but stood and motioned for me to follow. He led me to his office, where he began to dig among the piles of papers. Buried under one stack, he found what he had apparently been searching for. It was a small, soft-leathered sack. The mouth of it was tied tightly with a saffron-colored cord. Stegthal's fingers swiftly unknotted it and bulged the bag open.

"Give me your hand," he ordered.

I stretched out my hand, but Stegthal gripped my wrist and turned my palm face up, and then he poured the contents of the bag into my hand.

It appeared to be a pile of ordinary rocks, rough-edged and common, but as I gazed at them, I could see that some held streaks of color. One had silver strands, another turquoise. Three of them were mottled with a pale orange-like marmalade and speckled by sparkles of something much like copper. I attempted to use my left hand to move the rocks about, but Stegthal scooped them up and dropped them back into their pouch.

"How many objects did you see?" he demanded.

I attempted to count them in my mind, but Stegthal's voice, sharper than usual, snapped, "Report."

"Fourteen?" I guessed.

"Wrong. There were nineteen. You did not observe them well."

"You didn't give me enough time, and I was going to . . ."

The warning in Stegthal's eyes told me I was undergoing Shapechanger training. I should not have argued.

"Forgive me," I stated quickly, in the prescribed manner of a woman admitting a fault.

Stegthal nodded and looked pleased. "Good. I have no time or patience for early training. I am gratified that Shaarvan completed that level with you."

YesterTide, I would have ranted at Stegthal's words, but Shaarvan had taught me the culture of the Shapechanger. Except when my temper ignored it, I remembered it well: *Wisdom lies in survival, and pleasing one's Shapechanger Lord is survival.*

"You will practice this," Stegthal ordered. He handed me the sack of rocks and steered me to a chair. "I will give you the same amount of time. Be prepared for *any* question I may ask."

And thus, Stegthal's training began. Shaarvan had always been demanding but more or less fair, I guess, but Stegthal was neither fair nor patient. He didn't raise his voice or punish me for failure, but lessons didn't end until he was satisfied. When the rocks were finally slipped back into their sack and pushed back under a pile of papers, I was so fatigued I could barely stand.

As we left the office, he barred my way. "Shaara," he addressed me, once more using my name with a startling emphasis. "Your mind is tired. That is good."

He paused as if considering. "You have pleased me. I shall allow you to blend with the others when they arrive, but you will guard your tongue."

Another strange-tasting meal was produced from the food machine, but a familiar fruit followed it, and the drink Stegthal gave me was especially pleasing.

When the others returned, I reclaimed my son and fed him some of the fruit I'd been given, mashed into a sauce. My bondmates had fed Shaarac earlier, but Shaarac was always an enthusiastic eater, and he happily adjusted to tasting something new.

The Shapechanger Lords stayed awhile and talked of the general news of Westla and of various inconsequential matters. At times, they lapsed into a language I didn't speak, and then my eyes watched them even more intently, wondering if they spoke of Altar or of Shaarvan. I heard neither name, but I'd often observed how skillful Shapechanger were at subterfuge.

That night, when the others left and I'd put Shaarac to bed, Stegthal ordered me to go to my room and sleep.

"Please, may I stay in Shaarac's room?" I asked, my eyes dropped submissively. Stegthal took so long to answer I finally looked up.

His eyes were regarding me. They were dark, like nimbus clouds before a rainstorm. "I am your *husband*," he stated. "You will sleep in my bed, and there will be no further questioning of the matter."

I kept on my dress that night as I slipped under the coverings. I worried that it might make Stegthal angry, but I liked even less the alternative.

I have only a vague memory of Stegthal slipping into bed. Apparently, he didn't wake me, but when my eyes opened in the morning, the first thing I saw was my dress lying in a heap on the floor.

Thankfully, Stegthal had already left the room. I picked it up, recycled it, and was pleased when I was able to program the clothes machine myself. I chose a different style of dress than Shaarvan would have allowed. It had fewer buttons in the back and needed no assistance. The dress was equally as modest as the other, but the material had more give to it, and I liked the feel of the softer material.

I programmed slippers with a heavier sole and was quite content with the springiness of them. I was delighted with everything except the lavender color.

I ran a brush through my hair, one I'd also downloaded, checked on Shaarac, and then not knowing what was expected of me, went to stand in the entrance of Stegthal's office. He was once again bent over a computer monitor, jotting down notes from what he was reading off the screen.

I made no noise standing there. I was happy to watch him from the safety of the doorway, but Stegthal turned to look at me. He smiled at me and said, "You have a more friendly greeting for me this Tide?"

He only teased. I knew I was not required to answer, but I kept my eyes down just to be safe.

"Come here, Girl," he commanded.

When I reached him, he stood and took my face between his hands. Then he pulled me gently towards him. His lips met my forehead, and he whispered, "I shall expect a token kiss each morning, Child."

I didn't attempt to pull away. My eyes still looked downward, but something in the way Stegthal shifted his body warned me I hadn't pleased him.

"I believe you are obstinate," he said.

I gasped. What had I done wrong?

"The dress that clothes you through the Tide is for others to see. At night, it will not be worn in bed."

Inadvertently, I let out an exasperated sigh.

"You would argue?" he demanded as his brow grew stern.

I wanted to protest, to remind him that I belonged to Shaarvan, but he was suddenly holding my arms, gripping them fiercely. Isandor, the man who had owned me on Freinana, had once held me just as Stegthal did. Only Isandor had taken pleasure from the bruises his hands had made. Would Stegthal, too, find pleasure in my pain?

I bit my lip and lowered my eyes.

"Good," Stegthal said as his hands dropped from my arms. "Awaken the baby, and we shall eat."

I kept my eyes on the floor as I left Stegthal's office, but I felt him staring as I walked away.

Stegthal, in his office/lab on Westla

Shaarvan warned me that the girl is complex. That is an understatement. She is as challenging as the most puzzling of conundrums. Her mind is a labyrinth, full of twists and turns — intricate and multifaceted.

Shaarvan said I would find his wife to be intelligent. Far more than that. She is exceptional. She is quick of mind and brighter than half the scientists I have argued with. When I made her labor with the Shandor stones, she fought me, as she does with everything, but when she found I would give her no peace until she gave me effort, she exceeded all my expectations.

Yet, with all that ability, it is her outbursts of passion that rule her mind. She is obstinate, more than any woman I have encountered, persistent in what she wants and demanding, even in the midst of her knowledge of my dominance. Yet, I think she has almost no control over the flare-ups. In fact, they seem to frighten her. I have seen how fearful she grows when she finds she has overstepped the line. We shall work on that. I shall teach her how to temper her flares.

Shaarvan implored me to be patient with her. He knew his wife's faults. I watched him when he commanded Shaara to thank us for our bonding. Spelon said Shaarvan should have beaten her. I did not agree, although I had cause to question Shaarvan's leniency. But he was right. There is a fragility to Shaara that is not seen at first. I shall not push her beyond her endurance. Her wounds are many.

Patience is not a quality of the Shapechanger, but I believe I hold more of it than many others. I shall be indulgent for a while. Besides, I have not had such a fascinating enigma in many, many Passes.

Her fluctuations, in particular, intrigue me. One moment, she is fire and belligerence, and then a look sends her into trembling compliance. And when her defiance ignores the warning, and she persists, the moment I would reprimand her, I find that her mind is running scenes with Isandor of senseless beatings and unjustified castigations. Then, I cannot reprimand her, for in her mind, I would only be following in his brutish footsteps.

She will require much study and concentration. I presume that if I can understand her more accurately, I will know what path to take with her. Yet, tapping her mind, which I have repeatedly tried, does not seem to help. She is as uncertain of her mind as I am. I think that observation and relaxed dialogue will bring clarity. I shall tread most softly.

Shaara, on the artificial planet, Westla

Shaarac had wakened, and I was feeding him when my bondmates arrived. Thedar immediately took the baby from me. It wasn't fair. I'd had so little chance to hold my son. I started to complain, but a warning headshake from Stegthal ended any protest.

I watched my bondmates all crowd around and tickle Shaarac's belly. He loved them so much. He was giving them all messy kisses. I contented myself with at least being free to watch. The males stayed only a moment and then headed for the door, carrying my baby and saying their good-byes.

I stood. "Please, may I go?" I asked, careful to turn towards Stegthal, letting him know it was his permission I requested.

"You will stay with me," Stegthal said firmly. I sat and watched them leave, Shaarac laughing as they carried him out.

As the door closed, I turned to look at Stegthal. "Do you keep me prisoner here?"

"You are being childish," he said, shrugging off the question. He picked up the remnants of our meal, tossed it into the recycler, and walked out of the room.

He hadn't ordered me to follow him. I stayed in my chair, glowering, wishing the door would open and one of my bondmates would signal me to come. Of course, that didn't happen, so I started thinking about the places I'd seen in Westla and how I wished I were free to explore. Did the door still have an electric field?

Almost with my thought, Stegthal returned. "Why do you sit there? We have work to do in the other room."

I sighed. "What work?"

"Do not touch the door, Shaara. Of course, it is keyed to prevent your exit, painfully so. Females never walk about unattended. You know that."

I sighed. Would Stegthal then keep me prisoner forever? His eyes softened. I risked a question. "Shaarvan allowed me to go with my bondmates. Won't you?"

"I am not Shaarvan. Adapt to it, my dear."

That Tide, the task he gave me, dealt with numbers. I had sequences with patterns to complete. Each time I assembled one correctly, a small bell chimed, and the numbers shifted into new forms. At first, I was intrigued, and I thought the challenge was fun, but the *game* had no ending. Whenever I stopped, Stegthal knew it at once because the little tyrant of a machine would give a discordant beep that informed him that my fingers and brain were idle.

"Continue," Stegthal ordered each time the machine squawked.

His attitude annoyed me, and the increasing difficulty of the sequences began to make my head ache.

At last, I rebelled. I placed the tiny apparatus down on the table and stood, hands on my hips. "Send me to my room. Force me to do computer drills. Anything but this. I refuse to do a single sequence more."

Stegthal looked up from his work. For a moment, his eyes were so blank I thought that he hadn't heard me, but he focused and said, "Refuse?"

A chill hit my body. I flashed contrition.

"*Refuse* is the wrong word. Forgive me," I said.

Stegthal rose, stretched, and walked toward me. He stood a moment, towering over me, staring down as if deciding my future. I kept my eyes lowered and tried to remember the feel of sunshine.

"Shaarvan told me you were rebellious," Stegthal said, turning me around and pulling my back towards him. His hands moved up to play with my hair. I had braided it that morning. Shaarvan would not have permitted me to do so, but I'd often worn my hair braided on Freinana. I preferred it back and out of my way. Stegthal didn't mention it, but he untied the braids, then ran his fingers through the strands.

"I have witnessed your defiance on several occasions."

Was he still angry about what I'd said? Was he taking my hair down because he didn't like it braided? Or because he was punishing me?

"Why do you resist me?" he asked. His lips were on mine before I could attempt to answer.

Isandor had forced me like this. I let my mind drift to the forest. The trees welcomed me. They embraced me gently, dropping down fresh leaves to cushion my fall. The fragrance of black, rich soil was mixed in with the smell of crushed leaves. I breathed in deeply and felt at peace, my face tilted upwards to the sky.

"Enough." A deep male voice broke into my fragrant world. I opened my eyes to find that Stegthal had carried me to his room. I was lying on the bed, and Stegthal sat beside me, his hand raised as if he were about to slap me.

When he saw my eyes open, he dropped his hand. "Do you truly think that I shall allow you to retreat from me?"

He was livid. I was suddenly back at my testing, the testing that Shaarvan had forced me to endure. Stegthal's lips were searing mine, his hand traveling across my skin, touching my breasts. I could feel the webbing on my body as he surrounded me with it. His fingers parted the lips of my secret realm, touching me there, probing me, bonding me.

It was a projection. I knew that, yet I couldn't break free, and as Stegthal's lips joined mine in the bedroom, I couldn't take refuge in my forest. The touch of Stegthal, the taste of him, was an awareness I couldn't escape.

My hands pushed upwards at his chest, attempting to thrust him away from me. My fingernails scratched at his face. My mouth tried to turn, and then, failing that, I attacked his lip with my teeth.

A stinging slap of his hand branded my face, and then Stegthal sat up, stared down at me with a look of amazement, and laughed. His hands trapped my wrists and brought them up behind my back. His body twisted slightly to avoid the knee that tried to lash out at him.

Still laughing at me, he readjusted his grip on my wrists so that only one hand held my arms still, and his leg swung across to anchor my lower limbs.

"Now what, Child?" he chuckled. "Your outrage is mere sport. It cannot dissuade a Shapechanger. It only entices, my dear."

"But a Shapechanger doesn't rape," I said, then burst into tears.

Stegthal groaned softly. He let go of my wrists and rose.

"Juvenile emotionalism," he said, pacing back and forth. "Embryonic flimsy." He sighed loudly and snapped at me. "Stop your tears, Child. You have made your point. Come here."

I looked up to see how angry he was, but Stegthal was already flashing a Second Warning at my being slow to obey. I bolted up. Then I stood, unsure how close I was required to go.

Stegthal reached out and pulled me against him. His arms wrapped around my body. I did not pull away from him. I knew, somehow, that I was once again safe. This time, the hands that caressed my back offered only consolation.

Chapter Three

Shaarvan, onboard a spaceship bound for Altar

I keep hearing Spelon's voice calling me a fool. How could I marry my wife off to another male? How could I leave her behind? He asked me that over and over.

Because I am a fool, I wanted to reply.

As my ship sped further from the one who held my heart, my certainty of it grew greater.

But I could not stop the ship. I could not return for my wife. Fool or not, I was bound by my honor. I must go to Altar and end the mad reign of my brother.

Shaara could not come with me. It was the same dilemma I had deliberated for a twelveTide. No matter how I asked the question, the answer was always the same. I had to go to Altar, and I must do so without my son and wife.

"Yes, I am a fool, Spelon," I said out loud, but there was no one to hear me. The ship was empty, empty as my soul.

Thenos, in the Palace on Altar

My mother seems to be adjusting to her new husband. It must be quite distasteful for Tevor to lie there in his bed and listen to their bedroom play. I am grateful my mother's sad eyes stayed my hand when I would have killed him like the others. What an appropriate ending for such a difficult and demanding father.

I have sent spies to Westla. They will search for people who have met my princess. I wish to know everything about her. I shall discover what her preferences are, the foods she eats most often, and the colors she fancies. Perhaps I shall even learn what made her *cry out* in the bedroom when my brother rode her.

I shall decorate the palace with the shades that delight her, have tapestries and curtains adorning every room where she walks, and seed the gardens with the most fragrant seeds. I shall do everything to please my princess, and she will smile at me.

Then I shall make her my queen and all the Commoners will be forbidden to gaze on her. Perhaps I shall keep her from the Shapechanger as well. Why should other eyes share the beauty of my princess?

Come to me, my princess. Come to me, my Shaara.

Shaara, on the artificial planet, Westla

Later, it was back to work as if nothing had occurred between Stegthal and me. The mathematical sequences were resumed, Stegthal saying that I must complete the whole set before I could stop. I worked on them for a while, but all the time, I kept wondering how many were in a set. The little bell had chimed only six times before I placed my elbows on Stegthal's messy table, sighed, and looked about the room.

The discordant buzz of the machine went off, informing Stegthal I was slacking off. I was ready with my plea for a rest break, but Stegthal either didn't hear the tattletale buzz or had decided to ignore it.

I watched him cautiously for a while. He seemed busy with his research. I was quite content to be ignored. I stared at the masks decorating the room. Stegthal had said they were images of nonhumanoids. I liked the fact that Stegthal displayed them openly. Westlans did not approve of things like that, believing that only Shapechanger heritage should line Westlan walls.

I started remembering how Shaarvan had teased me when I'd thought Altarians worshipped an alien fertility goddess. His teasing had once irritated me, but now I looked back fondly. I wished he were here to tease me again. The thought of his being so far away where I couldn't touch him or see him, or even hear his voice made me want to scream and run about the room like a crazy woman. I knew I would go insane if I thought about how long it would be before I could possibly see him again.

I controlled my mind and shifted to thinking about Freinana. Frieda had told me all about the Wheel of Change. Could the Wheel still be controlling me on Westla? Did the gods stay on only one planet? My life was certainly demonstrating the turbulence that the god Barquel was supposed to bring down on people. Did Barquel really offset every good thing with an equally bad one?

Was that why . . . ?

"Shaara, sit down," Stegthal barked at me.

I glanced over at him and then looked away. I was surprised to find I'd been pacing back and forth. I sat and plopped my elbows on the table. I solved one of the sequences again, but my mind was still probing Freinanan philosophy. Could Barquel be punishing me? Was the god rebuking my husband for his challenges of the gods? Did they send him away?

"Child," Stegthal said, interrupting. I turned to look at him. He was staring at me with the most exasperated look on his face. "There are no gods offsetting good things with bad, and Shaarvan's leaving you on Westla has nothing to do with Barquel or the Wheel of Change."

I sighed. I wished I didn't project. It made life so difficult. I hung my head and attempted the next sequence of numbers, but I couldn't concentrate.

How did Stegthal know it was not the Wheel of Change that took Shaarvan away? Did Stegthal mean that Barquel had no power over the Shapechanger because they were gods, too?

"Who told you the Shapechanger were gods?" Stegthal said, laughing.

He left his studies to come stand and glare at me. I scooted around to face him, trying not to notice his foot tapping away on the floor. It was rocking back and forth as if it would like to squelch either my thoughts or me.

I met his eyes cautiously. Surely, he would not find fault with me for believing differently than he did. "Everyone on Freinana knows the Shapechanger are descendants of the gods."

"Freinanans are ignoramuses," Stegthal countered, turning away in disgust. He stomped off to his research, and I began to breathe normally again. With the best of intentions, I started back on solving the stupid sequences.

But a moment later, Stegthal growled, stood up, and walked back to me. "Freinana is a primitive planet, Girl, so of course it is filled with superstitions. But you are Shapechanger. Why do you still wallow in such nonsense?"

"How else do you explain the turbulence in life? For every sweet moment, there is always a bad. How can it be so evenly meted out if there is not a god weighing it precisely? The Freinanans claim it is Barquel's scale of justice. Why do you assume that can't be true?"

Stegthal laughed. "Someone sure did a good job of brainwashing you."

I shrugged. There was no sense in arguing with someone who would not reason.

But Stegthal didn't let it drop. He stepped closer until he stood over me, looking down, watching my fingers searching for the correct sequence. Then, he bent down, draped his arms around my body, and kissed the top of my head.

"Easy, Child," he said, laughing when I reared up and almost fell off the stool.

He twisted me around, then squatted down, his hands on my legs, his face peering into mine. "Listen to me. Life is always turbulent, and not because of some star in space that fools like the Freinanans call a god. Your turbulence comes from Thenos, and no gods control him."

"Stegthal," I said, attempting to explain one more time. "Once, when Shaarvan flew his ship, Ywequi, the great blue sun, attacked us. Shaarvan conquered Ywequi and then waged a battle against all the other sons of Barquel. I was there, Stegthal. I saw it!"

"The suns are only stars, silly child. Huge, vast balls of gaseous heat. They are not gods."

"I know that, but I told you. I saw it, a battle between all the gods and . . ."

"You saw a ship go through hyperspace. There was no battle."

I studied Stegthal's face. He was not laughing at me anymore. He just looked sad.

"Stegthal, on Freinana, when the stars moved in the sky and the positions of the planets altered, there *were* changes in the nature of the people. Some of Freinanans began to drink. Others became violent. Some folks went crazy. It all corresponded perfectly to the Wheel of Change."

Stegthal smiled. "People alter themselves all the time. Give them a special excuse, and they transform themselves even more. There is a science that deals with the understanding of why people do what they do. I shall teach you. But first, we shall cover astronomy. Come, Child. I shall show you my telescope," he said, and in his enthusiasm, Stegthal almost pulled me off the stool.

"I already know astronomy," I protested as I was propelled forward. "I studied it in my home world, and then Shaarvan taught me more."

Stegthal's smile grew bigger. One lip curled up into a gentle sneer. "Obviously not enough," he said, giving me a tug towards his computer.

"I understand the orbits of planets," I told him. "I know about novae, eclipses, and gravity. Shaarvan explained about the way magnets work off the poles. I am not the idiot you think I am, nor am I a child, Stegthal, and I wish you would release my wrist."

His lips spread open, and his teeth flashed at me. His hand loosened slightly, but he didn't release me. "I told you why I call you *child,* and until you gain control over that temper of yours and learn to think rationally, I shall continue to do so.

"And if, *my dear Child*, I did not think you were intelligent, I would not be wasting my time with you. In spite of the fact that you are female, you are bursting with intellectual potential — current superstitions excluded, of course."

While giving his speech, Stegthal had pulled me the rest of the way to the screen. His hand pushed me down on the seat. His fingers lashed out to clear the monitor of its equations, and then a second, much larger screen was suddenly descending. It contained the night and the stars and all that I had seen from Shaarvan's ship as I gazed outward through the control room's front panel.

I couldn't help letting out a gasp of pleasure. Beside me, Stegthal relaxed and bent forward. His hands were once more on my shoulders, and I felt the weight of his body pressing down on me.

I started to panic but with my thought, the hands were suddenly lifted, and Stegthal, with the leap of an attacking cat, was pouncing on the stool where I had sat. He picked it up, brought it over, and plunked it down beside me. I glanced over at his face. His eyes were focused on the giant screen, and they were glowing with such an intensity of passion I felt close to him for the first time.

And so, I began my education in the world of Stegthal: solar flares, planets revolving in opposition, and mathematics so far beyond my understanding that my head began to swell and pound. For hours, I breathed it all in happily, wishing that, sponge-like, I could take in more, but at last, with my brain throbbing and Stegthal demanding me to answer question after question, I moaned and held my forehead.

"What in stars is wrong with you now, Girl?" Stegthal demanded.

I couldn't think of an adequate answer. All I could do was cry.

My bondmates chose that moment to return. The first sound they heard upon entering was my sobbing and Stegthal's irritated voice berating me.

Spelon was the first to come running into the room. His stride was an elephant in stampede. Both Stegthal and I turned to look.

"What are you doing to Shaara?" Spelon demanded angrily, his face like a bull seeing red. I practically expected his foot to turn into hooves and to see him pawing the ground, readying his charge.

Tenor was right behind him, only quieter. He attempted to pull back his friend. "Let them be, Spelon. Stegthal is her husband now. You cannot interfere."

Spelon's face was set. He threw off Tenor's arms. His body took the Warrior stance, and his eyes glinted dangerously. "Why have you made Shaara cry?" Spelon bellowed in full challenge.

Stegthal didn't answer. He jerked me up, threw me back behind him, and took up the Warrior's stance as well.

I think Tenor had decided it was time for him to back up. He was retreating, still urging Spelon to come with him, when Thedar came striding into the room.

"Shaarac is asleep, Shaara. I put him down in . . . " Thedar froze, lapsed into silence, and stared at the two battle-ready Warlords.

I couldn't see much of anything behind Stegthal, but I could feel Stegthal's body all tensed up. His legs had crouched lower than normal and spread wide, and he was leaning forward like a tiger, ready to pounce. I figured from the rage flying about the room that Spelon was doing the same.

When Stegthal had tossed me behind him, he'd let go of me. I took advantage of the fact and darted out the side. Then, I dashed between the two agitated males.

"Stop it, Spelon," I cried out as I moved. "Stegthal has done nothing to me! You don't . . ."

"Hold!" The roar came from Stegthal. I paled. No Shapechanger made that sound unless he was half-Changed.

A furry arm caught me at my waist and scooped me back towards him, then twirled me about. My face slammed into his chest so hard the force of it knocked most of the wind out of my lungs.

The room had flooded with a dark yellow haze, and the odor of rotten pampa fruit permeated the air. Heated words were being flung over my head. Back and forth, they passed. I couldn't understand, but it no longer seemed important. I was fighting for breath. The arm that clamped me against Stegthal's body was cutting off my air.

The arm loosened, and air poured in, air as sweet as ice water when your throat was parched. I drank it in with huge gulps. For a moment, I felt reprieved. There was such great delight in being able to breathe. I was hardly aware of the shift of Stegthal's body, but his arms yanked me away from him and left me staring up into his fiery green eyes.

Fear swelled in my chest as I watched the Saberey's black diamond centers glare down at me. The coldness in a predator's eyes just before he strikes often freezes his prey. I was that prey, and once again, no air flowed freely into my lungs.

"I should beat you for your intrusion," Stegthal said, punctuating the sentence with a sudden shake of my body. "I would if I had not read in your mind that you are ignorant of the gravity of your offense."

I had not moved, but Stegthal grabbed my chin.

"You have violated several laws. To come between two Warriors in battle readiness was extreme foolishness. Had we not both been bonded to you, it could have resulted in your death."

I knew Spelon would not hurt me seriously. Did he mean that, as a tiger, he might lose control?

He shook his head. "Listen well, my little innocent. You will never interfere again between Warriors."

A flash of green from his eyes, a stab of pain in my head, and then it was done. I would never again forget.

The lesson over, Stegthal turned me around like a top, jerked my back up against his chest, and threw his arm about me in the Shapechanger hold, one rigid arm crossing between my breasts and locked at my waist.

Having dealt with me, Stegthal ignored my shaking body. Tensing his muscles almost back into the Warrior stance, he glared at Spelon. With iron spikes in his voice, Stegthal said, "I shall say this in the girl's tongue so she may also heed my words.

You are out of line, Spelon. Although I appreciate your concern for *my* wife, I must remind you. *She is mine to do with as I choose.* If you wish to honor the bond between the two of you, you will never interfere again."

There was a long silence. Thedar and Tenor nodded immediately. Spelon looked like he would dispute the claim, but his eyes traveled to his friends, and a look passed between them. Slowly, he turned back to Stegthal and gave his nod.

There was no friendly chatting in the large chamber that Tide. All three bondmates withdrew from Stegthal's chambers and did not return that night.

Teea, on her estate in Altar

My son Shaarvan has informed us he is returning to Altar. I am frightened for him. Thenos has declared Shaarvan, a traitor and says he will have his brother executed the moment he lands. Shaarvan must not come. I told him so, but he will not listen.

Starnkor spoke with him also. As my Second, Starnkor's role is head of our family, and as such, now he is Shaarvan's father. Shaarvan listened silently as Starnkor explained why he had taken possession of me. Then, my son welcomed my Second appropriately. (The two were as coldly formal as all male ceremonies on Altar.) They spoke of

Thenos and his edict. Shaarvan paid attention to Starnkor's words, but my son was not swayed by Starnkor's arguments. Shaarvan merely repeated that he would be arriving in two of our Tides.

The only good news was that Starnkor had the common sense to ask about Shaara. I learned that Shaarvan's wife had been Seconded and that she and their little son remained on Westla. Thank the Stars for that.

When our connection was broken, (Transmissions are usually kept short now so that spies are not able to break into them.) I wanted to discuss Shaarvan's arrival with Starnkor, but instead, I broke into tears and wept all over his shirt.

He did not scold me as Tevor would have done. He only held me, waited for me to calm down, and then said, "Be easy, Teea. It is not bad news. This is the catalyst we need, my dear. Do not fear for Shaarvan. We will fight for him. The others and I will not lose a Warlord like Shaarvan. There are too few of them left."

"But Thenos will . . ."

"No. Thenos will not get his hands on Shaarvan. It is time for us to build our defenses and our opposition. We shall prepare a well-guarded landing site for Shaarvan, and from there, our war against Thenos will commence."

War! Was it to be Shapechanger versus Commoner? Such a terrible thing, and one of my sons would probably die. I pray that it will be Thenos. May the fates forgive me for thinking such a thought, but it has become good versus evil, and we must all choose our side. Even a mother.

Shaara, on the artificial planet, Westla

The Tides drifted on. I heard nothing from Shaarvan, yet I missed him more each second that passed. Stegthal grew impatient with my daily question. One night, he erupted. "Enough," he growled at me. "You may no longer ask us if we have heard about your beloved Shaarvan. If we wish to tell you, Shaara, we shall do so, but you will not plague us with it again. I forbid it."

Stegthal's eyes did not flare cat-green with warning, but he had given a Shapechanger order. If I argued, I would be punished, and I had already learned that Stegthal never compromised. Stegthal was so sure of himself and of me that he did not wait to see if I complied. He and Thedar began a discussion of the proposed Oregian alliance.

I turned and surveyed the others. I had noticed that since the Tide of Stegthal's and Spelon's quarrel, Stegthal had taken over the leadership of the group. But this new command of his was so unjust, I was sure the others would counter it. Yet, not even Spelon looked up.

I walked towards the doorway, planning to go check on my probably still-sleeping son. Stegthal's voice halted me. "Come here," he ordered.

That was the very last place I wanted to be. For one second, I thought about ignoring his order and marching out of the room. Perhaps I'd tackle the outside door and check its voltage. But instead, I turned to look at Stegthal. His eyes had only the slightest hint of green, but without volition, my feet moved me towards him. He was leaning on top of a floor pillow with his legs stretched out on both sides. Once I was near enough, Stegthal's hands reached up and pulled me down into his lap. With his arms wrapped around me and his legs surrounding me, I fit compactly. I sat stiffly, not wanting to inhale the warm scent of him.

"Let the anger go," Stegthal whispered in my ear.

I wanted to tell him that if the anger went, the misery would set in. He read my thought and again, he whispered, "Let them both go, Shaara."

Later, when Shaarac woke up and began to wail, I tried to release Stegthal's arms so I could go to my son.

"Spelon," my Second said. "Would you do the honors of tending to Shaarac's needs this time?"

"Why?" I said.

"Quiet," I was ordered. "You still simmer in anger. Release it as I told you."

I let out a teakettle's hiss and then, without warning, burst into tears.

Stegthal turned me gently, and I sobbed my anger into his shirt. Tenor brought me a cloth to blow my nose, and I did so, but for a while, the tears dribbled. When only an occasional dry sob of misery was left, Stegthal turned me around and pressed me back against his chest. My head fit perfectly into the space he provided.

At first, I tried to listen to Spelon and Tenor playing with my son, but Stegthal and Thedar resumed their conversation. The voices mingled like background noise, calm and peaceful. Stegthal's heartbeat sounded louder than their voices. It galloped across the fields. Crimson Black, with legs stretched out, pounded away the distance. His hooves carried the beat, one-two-three, one-two-three, striking on the soft, dry dirt.

When I woke, it was morning. I lay there a moment, trying to remember where I was. I'd dreamed I was on Earth, getting ready to swim in the high school pool. I'd just squeezed into my swimsuit when a tall male walked into the locker room. I told him he couldn't be in there, but he just kept staring at me with his dark green eyes. "Come to me," he said.

It was only a dream, but it seemed important to recall those eyes. They weren't Shaarvan's or Stegthal's or any of my bondmates. I yawned and sat up.

Then I remembered the evening before, much more meaningful than a dream. I recalled how I wasn't allowed to ask about Shaarvan anymore. I searched for my anger, trying to call it up, but I could only find resignation. Maybe I really had been plaguing everyone, as Stegthal had put it.

I tossed the coverings back over the bed for the bed machine to straighten and went to pick out a new dress. Again, I tried my hand at designing. I patched in a dark lavender lace from a dress I thought was ugly and combined it with a simpler version of what I'd worn the Tide before. When the machine processed it, I was pleased with the result.

I left the majority of my hair unbraided, but I programmed the machine for a matching ribbon. I wove that into a small braid on each side, then connected them to lay on top of my unbound hair. As usual, I wished for a mirror, but Shapechanger didn't use them.

I found Stegthal in his office, bending over the small screen he preferred for his research. I greeted him and gave him the required good morning kiss.

His eyes passed over my hair, and he burst out laughing. "What is this — more Freinanan foolishness?"

I backed away. "It is a Terran style, and if it did not come out properly, it's because you Shapechanger are not technologically advanced enough to have mirrors."

Stegthal's eyes lit up with mischief. He stepped closer. "Do you not know what the Shapechanger say about saucy females?"

I didn't, but observing the look in Stegthal's eyes, I took another step backward.

He laughed. His hand shot out and grabbed mine and tugged me up against his body. His fingers immediately fondled my hair, unwinding the lavender ribbon and freeing the braided strands. "There. Now, enough of that silliness. You are Shapechanger. Do not attempt to take advantage of the absence of Shaarvan again. And the Shapechanger saying, my dear, is this: 'She who wears a biting tongue needs a husband's husbandry.'"

"I don't know what that means," I said, jerking away. "May I go get my son now?"

"Temperance, my dear. You are running out of time. Your Shapechanger body will soon require husbanding."

"Time?"

"A Shapechanger female cannot endure long without a mate, Shaara."

I ducked under his arm and moved toward the door. "I will wait for Shaarvan. He will return. You said so."

"Not even the strength of *your* will can endure that long," Stegthal said. "Yes, go, now. Tend to our son. Bring him to the eating room. He needs to begin taking meals with us.'

I stood outside the door of Shaarac's room, leaning my head against the outer panel. I listened for sounds that would tell me Shaarac was awake. I didn't hear any, so I closed my eyes and thought about what Stegthal had said.

Husbandry, was that just a fancy word for doing what Isandor had done? Was Stegthal warning me that he would soon be forcing me to do more than sleep in the bed we shared? Is that what he meant by saying I was running out of time?

Every night, when I got in bed, Stegthal's arms pulled me close to him then held my head on his chest. At times, his hands played with my hair or caressed my face. His body was warm and strong — like Shaarvan's, but even in the dark, the feel of him was wrong, his touch askew.

At first, I'd fallen asleep each night, concentrating on forcing the air in and out of my lungs, fighting my body's desire to match my heartbeat to Stegthal's. Then, in the mornings, I'd rise up angry and curse my traitorous body for letting sleep blot out the panic of my heart.

Stegthal had been patient with me. I knew this. Only once had he shown his anger. That had been the first night he'd come to bed before I was asleep. While he was disrobing, I'd childishly thrown the covers over my head and retreated into my cocoon, but Stegthal's arms had insistently untangled me. The battle that followed had panicked me. The strangest part is that I had not thought once of Shaarvan, only of Isandor.

Isandor was the man who'd owned me on Freinana. He'd had me first in front of the slaver who was offering me for sale, sampling me as if I had been a fruit to taste. He'd found me dry and unwilling, but he had bought me anyway. Then, for the quarterPass that followed, he'd cursed me and beat me for my coldness.

Later, he bought a pain stick that caused me unbelievable agony. But by then, he'd found pleasure in the bruises he inflicted with his fists. I'd sought the oblivion of death, and it had only been Tren, my friend, who'd taught me there was a reason to live. Tren and the landoor, Crimson Black.

But when Stegthal pulled me towards him, it was Isandor back in my bed, and I trembled like a frightened Earth deer being chased by a wolf.

"Easy, Shaara. I will not hurt you," Stegthal had said. But I'd fought him, a tigress in the jungle, attempting to draw blood with nails and teeth. When Stegthal wrestled me still, and I lay panting in my sweat, I heard his voice repeating over and over, "I am not Isandor. I am not Isandor."

Since that time, Stegthal had been gentle with me. Yet, I found myself growing angrier each Tide, incensed by the increasing familiarity of a chest that rose and fell beneath my ear, a heart that beat with a different gallop than Shaarvan's, and the sound of Stegthal's breathing, an alien tune in my inner ear.

I no longer craved sleep now as I'd done at first. For hours each night, I lay stiffly, fighting Stegthal's rhythm. Only when he slept was I free to curl away and hold my pillow in my arms. Then, I could pretend it was Shaarvan and remember the feel, the smell, and the taste of my husband. Only then could I sleep.

Now, standing in the hall of Stegthal's dwelling, I thought about my existence under my Second's dominion. What would I do if Stegthal moved forward if he chose to do what he'd told me was his right? I could not endure his touch. I could not betray Shaarvan.

Shaarac had started talking to himself. I loved to hear him coo and singsong. It jarred me from my thoughts. I remembered then that Stegthal would be expecting us. I moved forward into my son's room to prepare him for the Tide.

Thenos, in the Palace on Altar

They come! Shaarvan's ship has been spotted. How appropriate that he travels in a Westlan Ziper. That speedy little craft is the elitist of the Westlan super speeders. What could offer better proof of Shaarvan's traitorous ventures? How else could my brother have obtained such a ship when everyone knows he forfeited all his funds to finance his search for Shaara?

Now comes a major decision of my career. How do I handle Shaarvan's son? To order his death would bring the wrath of all. Yet, what good is the baby to me? The sight of him would constantly remind the princess of her dead husband. I suppose I must pretend to accept him. I remember how attached she was to the babe.

No, I'll have to do more than accept the brat. I must fawn over his exquisiteness to win Shaara's favor, which I will do, for a time. Every Tide, I become more proficient in my acting.

But how much time must I allow before the baby sadly sickens and dies? I shall want my own brat begun before too long, although I prefer Shaara's body to remain slender for a while. I shall give her a twentyTide before I make demands on her. That will allow her to get over her grief for Shaarvan and become acclimated to her new role. After that, I think, a halfPass, with the freedom to romp unaccompanied by a big belly, will be about right before I seed her.

I cannot help my smile. I feel so good. Everything is progressing smoothly. Soon, I shall feel Shaara's body pressed on mine. She will cry and fight me. How delicious that will be. I shall allow her tears. I shall encourage them. They will help her get over her fear of my arms around her. I shall pull her into my lap and cradle her like a hurt child. Progress will be slow with my princess, but in the end, she will be mine.

I dreamed of Shaara last night. She had clothed herself in the strangest garb. Her luscious limbs were unencumbered by cloth, and her breasts were full and bubbling over the top. A concrete pond sparkled with water. I think she was about to dive in. I spoke to her, and she to me. It was a pleasant dream. I could almost touch her.

Speaking of pleasure. My peons have brought me a sweet new delight. They have discovered that I am far more amiable to them when they keep me adequately supplied with new girls. This one looks a little like Goria. Her dark black hair will be a satisfying change from last week's blonde. That girl grew tedious with her huge green eyes forever a-sea with tears.

None of them have any spunk. If just one of them would stand up to me and rage like Shaara used to . . . Soon.

Shaara, on the artificial planet, Westla

The next Tide, when my bondmates arrived to take Shaarac, I turned wishful eyes at Stegthal, but I didn't ask to go. In all ways, I was an obedient and respectful Shapechanger wife, even as my bondmates departed with my son, and I was left behind once more.

Without a cross word or look, I stood and followed Stegthal into the office. I endured hours of lessons and accepted the trigonometry problems without argument. I'd finished them and had nothing more exciting to look forward to than more lessons when I stood up and spoke my mind.

"Stegthal, I have studied all morning and worked on mathematics until I have indentations on my fingers from using the criptor," I said, backing away from the table. "I have been doing my best to please you in everything, but does it have to be school every Tide? Can't we do something different? I'm bored with learning things."

Stegthal had been reaching up for a book when I began to speak. He lowered his arm and turned to watch me. "You have a vast amount left to learn," was his only comment.

I knew he was referring to my ignorance. His eyes followed me as I crossed the room and came towards him. "I have Passes to learn the rest. Please, let's go do something different," I begged, pulling at the sleeve of his shirt.

Stegthal rested his hands lightly on my shoulders. His eyes considered me. "I have felt your restlessness for Tides, but I do not have toys to entertain you."

"That's unfair." I almost stamped my foot before I remembered to modulate my anger.

"I suppose," he said, nodding after a moment, "It is possible that your youth makes you unable to sustain long periods of study."

"Why do you always talk like that?" I said, throwing my arms up in the air. It was a gesture that Shaarvan had tried hard to break. Shapechanger do not use unnecessary movements. My face probably turned hues of red. I jerked my hands back down. "You talk like an old man, Stegthal, but you can't be that much older than I am. How many Passes do you carry?" I asked, carefully using the Altarian phrasing rather than the Freinanan's.

"I shall not allow you to go freely about in the city if that is what you are asking," Stegthal said, ignoring my question. As if that ended it, he reached out, took my hand, and led me out of the office.

Stegthal had decided to break for lunch. I was surprised when, as we were dining on Slaemen, something that looked distinctly like raw squid tentacles, he resumed the conversation, or at least the part of it he was willing to discuss.

"Tell me. How do you prefer to be entertained?" he asked, slinging a Slaemen onto his tongue.

I shuddered and tried not to look at my plate full of them. When I picked up one, I found it to be just as slimy as it looked. I wished again that the Shapechanger policy of males serving and females eating whatever was served was not the rule. Stegthal slung a second Slaemen onto his tongue. He pointedly looked at my untouched plate. His eyes did not look open-minded about my dislike of his choice of meal.

"My first choice would be to ride landoors, but I'd guess that Westla doesn't have any," I said, and I tossed a Slaemen onto my tongue, shuddering and swallowing at the same time. The Slaemen didn't go down well. I coughed until I could breathe again then washed it down with juice.

"Obviously, the Slaemen is to be chewed, Shaara, and riding Landoors is not something that is going to happen."

I drained half of my drink before I could look up without gagging. "My bondmates were teaching me how to ski," I offered eagerly.

"Very useful," he said, dripping sarcasm. "Continue your meal, Child."

I stared at my plate. Perhaps it wasn't really like tentacles. Maybe, Slaemen were more like overcooked asparagus. I picked up another piece and dangled it. If you forgot the slime part, the eggplant color on the sides was interesting. My fingers twirled it for examination. Some parts of it were as shiny as a fly's body in almost the same luminescent green. The thought of the fly's body didn't entice me to ingest the food either.

"Interesting analysis, but your lunch is not a science experiment, my dear. Eat and continue to enlighten me as to your inclination for entertainment."

I shut my eyes and tossed the Slaemen slime-digit into my mouth. Over-cooked asparagus, over-cooked asparagus, I chanted mentally. I chewed briefly, swallowed, then drained the rest of my glass.

Stegthal raised his left eyebrow, scooped up my glass, and took it for a refill. When he placed the filled glass beside my plate, he didn't comment.

"On Freinana, I learned to bake bread," I told him. I wanted to mention that my bread was a lot better than his choice of meals, but Stegthal was obviously enjoying his Slaemen.

"The food machine takes care of all our needs," he informed me. When he looked up, I saw he was chuckling, probably reading my mind again.

His eyes seemed to be mocking everything I'd said. I decided to machine gun it. Maybe if I talked fast enough, I could give him a whole list before he cut me off. "I love to swim and ice skate. It would be great fun to see a play. Tenor saw one recently and said it was well-presented.

There is a wonderful zoo with animals from hundreds of planets. I would love to go there again. To climb over on the Zertted Ridge would be an experience! Thedar said you could see the whole city from up there. I can't imagine that.

I'd like to see my friend, Brala. Shaarvan, let us get together once. I definitely need to resume my training with Tessa. She's probably furious with me by now. And, there are lots of books I want to . . ."

"What books?"

"Shaarvan was letting me learn about architecture. When we visited different planets, we would locate the buildings by . . . "

"What other books?"

"Do you Shapechanger have *fiction*?" I didn't know the Altarian word, so I used the Terran one. Stegthal didn't respond. "Stories?" I explained. "Made-up ones."

"Inappropriate. Go on."

"Geology, astronomy, I guess. Everything from Altar is different than what I learned in Terran schools."

I felt like a horse on a lunge line, free to run unless I went in the wrong direction.

"Precise analogy," Stegthal said, smiling. He looked over at my plate. "The amount you have eaten does not match your nutritional needs, Child. Continue your meal."

I wondered how many slimies it took to meet my "nutritional needs." I grabbed up another Slaemen and poured it into my mouth. It's only fat spaghetti, I instructed myself. I chewed and tried to imagine that desperately.

"It is simpler to accept new tastes than to pretend they are foods you have previously known," Stegthal counseled.

I sighed and picked up another noodle. "Enough?" I questioned hopefully.

Stegthal shook his head and watched me deposit it onto my tongue. "I have listened to your words, Shaara," he said. "Many of your choices would not be wise at this time, but I shall permit your friend to visit you."

"Brala?" I questioned, figuring he would not be referring to the High Priestess as a friend.

Again, my thought amused Stegthal and his teeth flashed. He pushed his chair back and stretched out his legs. "No, I would not confuse the two," he agreed. His eyes continued to watch me as I ate.

My glass was again empty. "Please, Stegthal. I have satisfied my appetite," I said, using the Shapechanger phrasing for "I am full. May I stop?"

Stegthal raised a doubtful eyebrow. His eyes traveled from the plate to my face. He nodded. "You may recycle it."

When I returned and sat back down, his eyes looked thoughtful. "Perhaps Tessa's assistance would be helpful." He bent closer to me. "Why do you wish to continue training with the Priestess?"

The seriousness of Stegthal's eyes told me my answer was very important. I hesitated, searching for the right words.

"Reply," Stegthal ordered sharply.

"She helps me understand myself," I said hurriedly. It was not a Shapechanger answer, but Stegthal hadn't given me enough time to figure out precise wording.

He smiled distractedly and brushed his knuckles across my cheek. It was so much like one of Shaarvan's gestures I winced.

Stegthal's eyes noticed immediately. "It is not easy ascertaining what will heal you best, Child. Sometimes, an open wound needs covering. At other times, air heals it fastest. Your wound festers, no matter the prescription."

How had we gone from discussing Tessa to that? Yet I knew exactly what would heal me. "Bring Shaarvan back, and I will be well."

Stegthal sighed. His hand picked up mine. He turned it over and stared into the palm. When he started to lift it to his mouth, I attempted to pull away. He ignored my wishes and kissed the soft middle part of it. It was a form of Shapechanger magic. I knew I could not fight him if he continued.

"I would hate you always," I flared.

"You would get over it," he said, not bothering to meet my eyes.

"Never!" I reared up and backed from the table.

The pupils in Stegthal's eyes narrowed. I thought, at first, I'd pushed him into Change, but his eyes grew no greener, and I saw no shadow of the cat. Instead, it seemed he'd only withdrawn into his thoughts.

I flashed contrition. I knew I'd spoken too abruptly, too assertively. Was Stegthal now debating disciplines? Was he sorting through punishments to match my offense suitably? My fingers curled about the chair's high back. I loosened them and prepared to retreat.

Stegthal's hand lashed out, gripped at my hand, and then suddenly dropped it, allowing me my freedom. "Your fear is needless," he said. "I have taken no offense. Sit, Child."

I obeyed but sat on the edge of my chair. I knew a Shapechanger did not lie, but Shaarvan would never have allowed such willfulness to go unpunished. I was suspicious of Stegthal's ease with it.

He looked up. "My dear, I recognize the difference between willful and frightened, and as you well know, I am not your Shaarvan."

I let out my breath, but I did not change my position on the chair.

Again, Stegthal's eyes focused on me. "You are shaking. Relax, Child. If I were unsatisfied with your behavior, you would have felt my hand by now."

I hadn't been aware I was trembling until he mentioned it. I did a mental exercise that Tessa had given me. It helped, but if Stegthal had moved a couple of planets away, it would have helped more.

Again, his smile was back. "Yes, I shall let you work with Tessa, although I am not interested in whether she helps you understand yourself." Once more, his hand stretched out to take mine. I didn't dare pull back again. I dropped my eyes and waited.

"The understanding you seek is defined only by your husband, Shaara. Tessa may tell you what answers she has found, but they are not yours. I shall permit her training only because it will help you to find temperance."

I didn't care what the reason was. "Thank you," I said, still not daring to look up.

"There is a matter that worries you a great deal, Shaara. It is better that I bring it out into the open.

"I have decided not to take you, not until you are driven by your need. I shall give you that measure of time for your mourning of Shaarvan. I believe you need it. But when the frenzy interferes with your health, my wife, then I shall force the issue."

"My need will always be for Shaarvan."

Stegthal shook his head. "No, Shaara. That is not true."

He stood and raised me up beside him. His eyes held mine. I could not look away. The green in his was a field of waving grass. I let him walk me through it. And when I turned to look at him, I saw the cat image shadowed in his face. It did not frighten me. It was only a dream.

"Yes, it is a dream," Stegthal told me, "a Shapechanger dream that you will remember when you wake. You are so easily frightened when I try to reach you. It seems a gentler way to inform you of what you do not understand. Listen to me, my lovely Shaara, my wife.

"You are Shapechanger now. If you wait too long before you accept your need, it will be the cat side of you that comes alive. A feline in heat accepts any mate, but she finds little pleasure in it. She is driven by the need and must be taken over and over.

"Listen to your body before you get to that point, Shaara. Come to me. It will be easier on you in your human shape than in full Change. Remember what I am saying to you."

His lips touched mine, and then the dream was gone, and I found that I was standing there staring into forest green eyes.

"You did that?" I asked in awe.

"I am Shapechanger."

"You are of the gods," I whispered.

Stegthal sighed and shook his head slowly. "Come, my wife. We shall call on your friend."

Chapter Four

Tenor, on the artificial planet, Westla

I do not agree with Spelon about Stegthal. Stegthal is doing a good job with Shaara. She is still nervous and brittle with the high tension of her loss, but Stegthal comforts her well. He keeps her busy with studies. If her mind is full, she cannot pine as much.

Stegthal has begun holding her with as much of his body in contact as possible. It is what she needs. Although I believe that taking her would smooth away some of her tension, I understand why Stegthal has not yet ridden her. Shaara's mind is full of Shaarvan. It pours from her thoughts in waves of sadness. Stegthal is by far stronger than I am. I know if Shaara had been my responsibility, I could not have borne to let her grieve so long. It wears on one's nerves.

Stegthal has stopped Shaara from asking about Shaarvan. In this, he has been wise, also. We are grateful because her little face takes on such wistfulness, and her eyes plead so sadly. It rips out your heart when she looks at you like that.

We would, of course, tell her if there were something positive to say, but there is no good news from Altar. I spoke with a male a quarterTide ago who had just left the planet. He told me Thenos had signed a death warrant for Shaarvan. It condemns him without judgment from the Elders. According to the warrant, Shaarvan is to be shot on sight.

I have discussed this with the others. We shall relay none of it to Shaara. She is better off with her memories and her hopes. Stegthal says Shaara is not strong enough to hear such news. Thedar speaks in favor of telling her. He says Shaara is stronger than we allow her to be, but I do not see that.

Thedar also informed us that Tessa is demanding we keep Shaara informed. But, of course, the decision is Stegthal's, so whatever our opinions, we shall not mention a word of what is happening on Altar.

Stegthal, the one who was always temperate and sensible, did not like hearing of Tessa's interference. I think he would have let his irritation be known if Shaara, sitting in Stegthal's lap, had not looked up at that moment and attempted to read him. (We have all noticed that she has grown more capable in that area. It requires that we maintain a shield against her at all times.) At Stegthal's insistence, the conversation moved away from the High Priestess' directive.

The other news we discussed (in Despegan, Spelon's home language, so that Shaara could not understand) is the conversation that Tem had with Spelon yesterTide. It seems that Westla is forming an army to be ready to assist Shaarvan in his war on Altar. Westla never involves itself in Altarian affairs, but the issuing of a death warrant against the heir (Has Shaarvan been officially proclaimed?) seems to have stirred them up. None of us may join. We are bound to Shaarvan's wife and son and, therefore, may not go to Altar. Such a pity for Spelon. He is quite depressed not to be included in the battle plans.

We did have some information that we could share with Shaara. Shaarac toddled for the first time. We thought that would cheer her up, but instead, she burst into tears. She was good about not speaking Shaarvan's name and how he had missed such an important event, but with her projection, we all heard it. It was an awkward time for us. Shapechanger males are inept in dealing with female tears.

Still, it was an amazing feat for little Shaarac. He is stronger than the average child of his age. His lineage will be proud.

I think Spelon forgets at times that Shaarac is not his son. Ever since we saw the baby's first step, Spelon has been swaggering, boasting that Shaarac will be a famous Warlord. I am sure that will be true. I also feel a father's smugness. It is hard not to feel ownership of a child we foster so closely.

The child does bear the signs of Power. Already, he challenges us in small ways. Shaarvan, if he lives, will have much to be proud of in his son.

Tren, on the artificial planet, Westla

When we finally arrived on Westla, both the captain and Targone escorted me to the Great Hall to see Tem, the First of Westla. It was an honor to be received by him, they told me. I wondered why a Commoner should rate such respect. However, I knew that Tem was Shaarvan's uncle. I supposed that he only wanted to thank me for Shaara's return.

The way was lined with corridor after corridor of marble halls. Shapechanger flowed all around us. I was more awed by their profusion than the thought of meeting the First of Westla. I have never been all that impressed by position.

As we walked, I continued my questioning. As before on the ship, neither Targone nor the captain seemed hesitant over providing information. I was delighted with such interesting details. However, when I asked about the number of Commoners on Westla, the captain's answer stopped me in mid step.

"There are many females, but male Commoners are not allowed on Westla," he said.

I halted. "Then why am I here?" I demanded, ready to bolt back to the ship.

Targone assured me that special permission overruled any such previous rules. "You saved Shaarvan's wife," Targone reminded me. "She is a member of the Trendacons, as is the First. I am sure that Westla is willing to forgive your Commoner blood in this case."

The captain looked a little bemused, but he nodded vehemently.

I let them lead me forward, but I was feeling more misgivings over the visit than before. Forgive my Commoner blood? If a whole ship of them had made me edgy, imagine what an entire planet of Shapechanger must feel like, especially if they all felt like that about Commoner blood.

We arrived at the audience hall soon after. Tem was sitting on a special chair, one that looked exactly like a throne to me, but Targone kept assuring me it was simply a chair. It was true that Tem wasn't dressed magnificently, and he wore no crown on his head. He looked like any average Shapechanger, at least one who towered over everyone.

I could feel Targone's awe. That told me more than words alone. I felt sorry for Targone when he began to stutter. I knew he had wanted to make a good impression.

At one point in the interview, Captain Jorvanel led Targone away, and I was invited to dine with Tem. I accepted the honor. I was hungry, and a conversation in a quieter environment than the great hall would be a big improvement. The two of us proceeded to a rather humble room where a very pretty young girl brought us fruits and plates full of varied foods. I was interested in the girl. Was she a slave or the wife of one of the Shapechanger?

Tem laughed at my question. "A wife would never be used as a servant. A wife is served by her husband. She is accorded every homage to her position."

I thought back to Shaara's halfPass with Flar and Frieda. She had not only baked and cleaned, she had done the serving most of the time. If only Tem knew, but then, perhaps he did.

The serving girl was lovely. Several times, her breasts touched my face as she placed dishes in front of me. Her hair flowed down to her waist. It didn't have the vibrant colors of Shaara's, but it smelled delightful.

"She pleases you?" Tem asked.

"She is pleasing," I hedged.

"She can service your needs if you like, at least until Shaarvan goes on another of his forays for fresh girls. He has told me that he promised you a wife."

I almost choked on the bite of bread I was chewing. The girl's eyes met mine. She was obviously no shy virgin.

I cannot remember if I answered Tem. My eyes had begun to flag, and my head was suddenly so heavy I could scarcely hold it up. I recall placing my drinking glass on the table very carefully so as not to spill it. That was my last memory of the meal.

Shaara, on the artificial planet, Westla

The next Tide, my friend's husband, brought Brala to Stegthal's quarters. After a cool greeting to me, the husband walked off to talk with Stegthal, and Brala and I were free to chat. We sat in the entertainment room and played with Shaarac. My son was all smiles and enchanted silliness. Brala said he reminded her of her son when he was a baby, and then she talked about her son's current studies on Westla.

It was pleasant having Brala's companionship. I had almost forgotten how relaxing being with females was — the easy smiles, the peacefulness. Even Brala's questions were gently given, and no demands came when my answers didn't settle her curiosity.

And then, my bondmates came in. They never arrived quietly. We heard the sound of an army platoon clumping towards us through the eating room. They stopped in the doorway of the chamber and almost collided with each other when they saw us sitting there.

"Where is Stegthal?" Spelon demanded, striding forward in front of the others. Spelon never relaxes. He holds to the Warrior's stance even when he eats or when we sit around in the evenings talking. His eyes were already scanning the room like he suspected he would find an assassin or a thief in the corners. Thedar and Tenor followed him in. They smiled their morning greeting to me.

"Stegthal is in the office," I told Spelon, and then I introduced them all to Brala.

Spelon barely let me finish speaking. "He has left you alone?"

I stood up, trying to hold on to my wiggling son. His hands were stretched out and flailing about. He was having a fit because he saw Tenor standing there and wanted to go to him. Shaarac was quite good at rotating favorites. Obviously, Tenor was the chosen one for this Tide.

It was a relief to hand over the struggling little body to Tenor, but I was disappointed when I tried to give Shaarac a kiss, and his hands pushed me away. My son wasn't talking yet, but the sound of his verbal rejection was an awful lot like "no."

Tenor smiled. "He will sing a different tune when he sees you this afternoon, Shaara."

I could feel Spelon becoming impatient with my failure to answer him. I turned to face him. "Spelon, as you can see, I am not alone. My friend is with me."

Spelon was still offended. His eyes glared at me for a moment before he turned to frown at Brala. "A woman does not count."

Spelon's body was massive. Even his head and face seemed larger than the others'. When he lifted his arm to pat Shaarac's head, the material of his shirtsleeve strained with bloated muscle. I was used to Spelon, but my friend was not, and Spelon's eyes, scowling at her as if she were the one responsible for Stegthal's absence, made her face grow pale. For a moment, I thought Brala might panic and run to her husband, but she stiffened her back and stayed, her eyes clinging to the floor.

"Spelon," I hissed. He turned to look down at me. His eyes softened.

"You are frightening Brala. Stop glaring at her. Please?"

The muscles in Spelon's face clenched. I thought he would lift me up into the air and shake me for being so bold. He growled deep in his chest. His hand reached out as if to touch my cheek, but before I could move back, he dropped his hand and whirled around to stare at the doorway as if worried Stegthal might be watching.

Thedar came up behind him, slapped the Warrior on the back, and laughed. "You frighten all of us at times, Spelon. Relax."

"Stegthal should not have left her with a woman. Shaara is still unstable."

I opened my mouth, but Thedar's hand flashed the silence command. "Keep your tongue a prisoner unless its words are sweet," he said. With the silence command on me I could not answer anyway, but Thedar's words probably saved me from a harsher scolding.

Tenor moved towards us, and then all three of them stood surrounding me. They no longer touched me since I had been wedded to Stegthal, but I could feel our bond. Their eyes watched me. I nodded.

"Shaara is doing well, Spelon," Thedar said, studying me. "There is little cause for your concern. Her friend may do her good."

Spelon growled again, his eyes scanning me. "I would not leave her alone," he commented to the others.

"We go now. Tell Stegthal we bid him good morning," Tenor said, jostling my son up and down. "He will know we have Shaarac."

My son held out his arms to me, and I got my kiss after all. Even Spelon's eyes turned mild as he watched. Then, each of my bondmates inclined his head briefly to Brala and me and left as noisily as they had arrived.

When I went to sit down beside Brala, her eyes had grown enormous. "I knew you were different than the other wives," she said, "but to have four Warlords so intimately close to you. How is that possible? And with your Second husband in the other room . . . Why does he permit this?"

"They are bondmates," I answered her, but I was uneasy discussing them. The testing that had bonded me was a subject I was forbidden to discuss. I did not think I should say more.

"How do you tell them apart? They are all Warriors, padded with muscles and fierce expressions. The three of them resemble each other in a way. Every one of them is nightmare-producing," she joked.

I laughed. "I think you're remembering Spelon. He always glowers. He's the one who looks ready to battle monsters — or unruly females."

She giggled. "Yes, I know which one you're describing. And the others? Are they as bad?"

I shook my head and offered her a refill on her half-empty cup of Kuhla. She declined and waited for me to continue.

"Tenor is the oldest. He has streaks of gray in his hair, which is quite unusual for a Shapechanger, I've been told. He's rather sweet, actually. Thedar, well, he's not bad, either. He's always lecturing me about my behavior, but he does it in a gentle way. He's the one with heavy, kind of shaggy eyebrows."

"But not unattractive."

"No, all my bondmates could have been supermodels in my home world. Did your planet have something like that, where the most handsome men showed off clothes or products?"

She laughed but shook her head. No, we were big on androids. They exhibited fashions whenever someone wanted to display more than one outfit, although most of us simply designed our own daily wear. It was a status thing, displaying our Tide's costume. Some of the males and females seemed to enjoy shocking society. Others merely rotated an outfit's color. But fashion was a major part of the daily gossip. On my planet, people were always rather vapid and shallow.

"But back to your guardians. Tell me about the head warrior guy. What's his persona? Does he always growl?"

I shot a glance at the door, checking that our conversation was still private. "He's next in line. The back up of the backup, I guess you could say. And he constantly reminds me of the fact. If Stegthal ever . . .Well, Spelon likes to think he's in charge of me, even though he's not. Oh, and he's Warrior Elite, whatever that means."

Brala nodded as if she understood. She reached for another Spoola fruit, chewed it, and swallowed. "I love these," she said. She waited a moment, thinking over what I'd said.

"Is bonding on Westla part of the testing then?" she asked.

I kept my head down and didn't respond. I wanted to tell her everything. It had been so long since I'd had a friend, at least in the Shapechanger world.

"Shaara!" Brala protested. "Not you, too. What are you afraid of? There are no Shapechanged Lords here now. How can they beat you for something they don't know about?"

I didn't look up or speak.

"All right! We will change the conversation," Brala said as her hands moved up to comb her long black hair. She twisted its fullness into a bun and tucked the ends inside. Her eyes darted to the doorway almost fearfully. Then, she laughed at herself and made a male gesture of disrespect. I gasped at her courage.

"Tell me why Shaarvan is not here," she said, letting her silver slippers drop to the floor and then curling her feet up on the floor pillow.

I flashed a quick look towards the doorway. I admired her bravado, but I didn't want to get caught in the fallout.

"Relax," she told me. "I assume the outer door is locked?" I nodded, and she continued. "Then they have no reason to check on us."

"But . . ."

"Don't tell me you obey every command of your new husband. Does he have you that frightened?"

Her question also made me feel uneasy, but I couldn't help saying, "You're not afraid of yours?"

"Sometimes. Let's just say I'm cautious, as all good Shapechanger wives are. But, I thought we were going to talk about Shaarvan — that gorgeous hunk!"

I tried to ignore her praise of Shaarvan. He would have been furious to hear Brala speak of him that way. Only males talked like that, and only about girls who were not Shapechanger wives. A Shapechanger wife would be beaten for saying she admired a male's body. I wondered how lenient Brala's husband was.

"Shaara, wake up! Where is Shaarvan? Why is he not here?"

"He returned to Altar," I told Brala, sadly. "Stegthal tells me there is a war there. I miss him so much, and I worry that . . ." I used the cloth hanky Stegthal had given me. I keep it with me all the time now, watering it daily.

Brala slipped her arms around my shoulders. "Stop worrying, Shaara. Worry can't change anything except to make you ill. Your Shaarvan is safe. Keep thinking that. Don't allow fear to enter your thoughts."

"I'm sorry," I said, sniffling. "I had forbidden myself to cry while you were here. I used to be able to shut off tears and think of other things. Now, tears build up inside me, and I feel like I am drowning in them."

"As if there were a weight crushing you down?" Brala asked, looking at me oddly.

"Yes!" I gave her a quick hug. "Thank you for understanding."

The same strange look met my eyes when we pulled apart. "I do understand, Shaara, but it is not the missing of Shaarvan you are describing."

"What do you mean?"

"Why has Stegthal not bedded you?"

"Brala, not you, too!" I said and bolted up and away from her. I took two steps across the flooring and then swung back to look at her.

She was sitting there calmly, with those eyes that had drawn me to her from the first, eyes that seemed to know more than I could ever hope to learn.

"I'm sorry," I said. "I didn't mean to give insult."

"Shaara, I'm not a male," she said, laughing. "I won't beat you for displaying a spark of anger. I understand exactly what you're feeling because I've been there."

She patted the seat beside her, and I came back and sat back down. I knew she had a story to tell me. I hoped it would help.

Brala shook her head, and her eyes looked across the room as if the story were written on the wall. She took a long, deep breath, and her voice, strained with the emotion of what she was about to tell me, was at first scratchy and weak.

"My husband once flew to Blegor for a twentyTide," she began. "He refused to take me with him because he said it was dangerous there. Before he left, Shaara, he bought a male slave, and he ordered that slave to . . . to pleasure me."

Suddenly, her voice gave out, and she breathed in sharply. She looked down at her fingers, all twisted and white from the pressure of her grip. I reached out and took her hands in mine. I knew all about being forced to do things against your will. It was a link all females shared. Brala's eyes met mine. She drew a breath and steadied herself.

"It wasn't just that the slave . . . He watched me, Shaara. My husband webbed me so I couldn't resist, and then he watched that slave take me. Do you understand what that was like?"

Once more, her eyes flew to mine. I nodded, and she continued. Her voice had grown stronger. She was over the part that hurt the most. The rest came easier. "I have never forgiven my husband for it, Shaara, not that it makes the slightest difference to him. If he were going back to Blegor again, I do not doubt he would choose another slave to stay with me."

I closed my eyes a moment. I was feeling for Brala, yet remembering the times that Shaarvan had hurt me in similar ways.

Brala was right. Sometimes, we could not forgive, and the fact that we harbored that pain in our souls, and they didn't care that we did, hurt even worse.

"After he left me, Shaara, the frenzy came over me. I couldn't eat or sleep. That slave saved my life."

I shook my head and looked down. It wasn't that I didn't believe Brala, but I knew it wouldn't be like that for me. "I would die if someone besides Shaarvan touched me in that way," I told her. "It happened once . . . on Freinana. I will never allow it to happen again."

Brala smiled. Her eyes were kind, but they held amusement. "You are Shapechanger, Shaara. It is inevitable."

Again, I shook my head. "No, it isn't. I lived on Freinana for many, many Tides without a male."

Brala sat back against the wall. She stared at me in disbelief. Then, her eyes became thoughtful, and I could see she was trying to figure out the explanation. "I've never heard of anyone doing that. How did you sleep?"

Her eyes were so puzzled I almost laughed, but I was afraid that instead, I'd end up crying because there was really nothing funny about either of our plights. Besides, her story was too close to what Stegthal had said in that strange Shapechanger dream.

"Wait," Brala cried out. "Freinana is where you lived when you were mindwiped, isn't it? And you'd never Shapechanged at that point, right?"

I nodded. I didn't understand why that was significant.

"Don't you see, Shaara?" Brala leaned forward, almost rising, she was so excited at having solved the mystery. "You were not fully adapted then. That's why you survived it! But you have Shapechanged now. You are one of them . . . " She flushed and corrected herself. "I mean, you are one of us."

I smiled, forgetting her solution as I thought about her verbal slip. I knew exactly what Brala meant. The males had been born Shapechanger. They'd grown up in their heritage, while we females had only been altered, taken from our native cultures, and forced into strange new customs.

Brala had been with the Shapechanger many Passes longer than I had, but she still felt only partially Shapechanger. It was still *them* and *us* for her. Would we always feel that way, even after raising a son and spending our life with the Shapechanger?

While I was thinking, Brala continued talking about the signs of the frenzy. I was glad I tuned her out. I changed the subject as soon as it was polite to do so.

Tem, in the Palace of Westla

Shaarvan left his wife here and returned to Altar. Although it is best, I could not help but feel his pain. His shielding was weak at the ceremony of her Wedding. And the woman — she was a raw sore, oozing misery. It was not the happiest occasion for any of us who witnessed it. Perhaps it is a forewarning of what is to follow. There will be little happiness, I fear, as the war on Altar escalates. Too many of us on Westla have family there.

Shaara's bondmates are keeping me informed of her health and well-being. I am not surprised that she is having trouble adapting. She is a strong-willed woman. Tessa has told me that Shaara will be a Priestess one Tide. It is good that Shaarvan has wedded her to a strong-minded Warlord. Stegthal will need to be decisive with her and extremely patient.

The Commoner who notified us of Shaara's whereabouts on Freinana has been taken for transition. I agree with Shaarvan. Tren has raw power. I do not know why such individuals appear at random in the population of the Commoners. Without genetic alteration of any kind, their genes should not carry the attributes of the Shapechanger. It is a curious evolution. When we find such a man, we always claim him for the Shapechanger.

This one should have been marked earlier. We should have caught him sooner. How was it that he blended in with the Freinana and yet learned so much about us without being noticed? Why was he never tested?

We must strengthen our nets. Our searches must be increased. It would take only one of these genetic mutations to destroy all we have built. If one like Thenos can do so much damage, imagine what a nonShapechanger with Power could do. Without our codes, the training, and the laws that give us guidance, Power can be a heady experience. It can destroy.

Tren is young. What would he have done when he became bored with living the life of a Commoner? He bonded Shaara. He used the Patterns. I shudder at such knowledge and Power in the hands of a Commoner, but he seemed to have been cautious and did no other harm. We were fortunate. He shall add important traits to our gene bank. We shall study him and the attributes he brings us. Ours must not be a stagnant race. We must continually forge our way higher on the path of the Stars.

Shaarvan has given us permission to use his own DNA on the man and then foster him. Already, Shaarvan has written Tren into our family line, and we shall give him suitable training for his new position. If he does not resist, it will not take long to incorporate him into our world.

How advantageous the misfortune of Shaara and Shaarvan brought us such a windfall. The Old Ones are quite ecstatic over the man's wild, mutant genes. They are impatient for his adaptation to be completed so they can delve into his mind and see what the meld has created. Yet, they have promised they will not stifle him. As Tessa said, "Tren *must* be allowed to fulfill his path," (although it seems to me that our intervention has already altered that considerably).

It is remarkable to consider that when Tren completes his transition he will be my nephew. I think I shall like him. He seemed an intelligent and personable man when he was a Commoner. When he wakes, I shall give him whatever guidance he is receptive to. I hope he can progress through his anger quickly, but it is likely he will not be pleased by the honor we have given him.

Pathe, in the medical offices on Altar

They have let me join the Resistance. I am delighted. Although my skills do not help them now, since I do not know a pipe weapon from a hunting pipe, at least I shall be able to serve as a medic when the actual fighting begins.

I am impressed with the way that Mother has taken a leading role in the campaign. Of course, they will not allow her to expose herself to the violence that is to come, but they have permitted her to learn the tactical maneuvers and to discuss them as if she were one of the males. I think Starnkor has been good for her in this respect. He encourages her, and he stands at her side during every argument that ensues when she speaks out against some policy they have always had and wish to continue just because they have always done it that way.

Mother is amazingly level-headed, and she speaks with a gentle confidence that surprises many of them. I know they expect her to break into tears when they glare at her, and several times, they have flashed signs at her, but again, Starnkor, at her side, urges her to continue, and she valiantly does. Bravo, Mother!

It will not be easy to war against the Commoners. We have resisted doing so for thousands of Passes. We knew they could not stand up to us, so what was the point? Yet, they have driven us to the realization that it is not enough to have the potential to do a deed—sometimes, one must actually perform it. I am ready. After what they did to Goria, I do not feel the reluctance I once would have.

I have met with the Resistance four times now. I shall not write down a single one of their plans because there are spies everywhere. But I must say I am proud to be a part of the war. When Shaarvan arrives, I know he will lead us to victory.

Shaara, on the artificial planet, Westla

When the door to Stegthal's office whished open, Brala gave her head a couple of violent shakes. The silky hair dropped down neatly around her face. Her feet were already shoving themselves back into dainty silver slippers before the footsteps outside the doorway of the central room gave notice of anyone's approach. I gave my friend a thumbs-up, and Brala laughed.

I stood up as the males entered. It was not the custom here, but my Altarian training often overruled the more lax traditions on Westla. Having an Altarian husband probably had much to do with that.

Brala raised her eyebrows and shook her head. "Shaara," she hissed at me.

Her husband walked forward, and Stegthal followed. "Brala, stand up," Braltar demanded. "I expect the same graciousness in you as Stegthal's new wife displays."

I would have apologized to my friend if I'd been allowed to speak. I hoped she'd forgive me. I hadn't meant to get her in trouble.

"Raise your eyes, Shaara," Stegthal commanded, obviously pleased by Braltar's praise. I looked up, wondering what was expected of me.

Brala's husband made it clear. He asked for permission to touch me. My eyes flew to Stegthal. *"Please don't,"* I pleaded silently, but Stegthal agreed to Braltar's request.

Bralta's hand caught my chin, lifted it slightly, and turned my face towards him. He inspected me a moment as if I were a girl he intended to buy. The procedure was not uncommon, but its past occurrences didn't make it any easier for me to endure.

"She is an amazing projector, Stegthal. Even with her face placid and accepting, her anger has a molten force. I can see she is healthy. Her hair is shiny, and her skin has that translucent clearness of proper nutrition. It is obvious you are taking excellent care of her. Shaarvan will be well pleased."

With his assessment complete, Braltar lost interest in me. He released my chin and moved towards his wife. "Come, Brala," he ordered. He used his arm to secure his hold on her and then turned back to Stegthal. "Your work is extraordinary. I look forward to analyzing the data you gave me."

Brala and I could say nothing in parting. A female could never initiate conversation in the presence of a male she wasn't bonded with, so we merely traded furtive farewell smiles.

I watched as my friend and her husband departed through the outer door. It had been pleasant (and informative) talking with her. I wondered when we'd be allowed to visit again, but I had little time to consider the thought. Lessons resumed immediately.

Stegthal was either in a generous mood that Tide, or else he wanted to get some work done without me around to disturb him. That afternoon, when my bondmates came home with Shaarac, I was given permission to go to Tessa's for training.

The freedom I felt as I stepped through that outer door was an even greater treat than Brala's visit. It was worth having to listen to Stegthal's lecture about the conduct he expected of me and having to give my word that I'd obey the orders of my bondmates.

Our walk to Tessa's was short. Spelon only once upbraided me, and that was hardly my fault. We'd walked by five young Shapechanger. They were only youths and should have been ignored. But Tenor got angry when they followed behind our guards, talking loudly about what they'd do if they owned a female like me.

It was actually the only time I'd ever seen Tenor fume. He stopped, and Thedar, Spelon, and the guards who still accompanied me whenever I left our residence all spun around, ready to do battle with boys closer to my size than theirs. I figured I was supposed to turn, too, and how could they expect me not to watch?

Tenor tossed some very harshly spoken words at the boys in a foreign language. Either the boys were put off by something he said, or else they didn't like the odds. They ran off.

It was all quite fascinating, but Spelon became irate that I'd looked up. He accused me of having flirted with the boys to attract their attention. I might have popped off with something that would really have gotten me in trouble if Tenor hadn't immediately given me the silence command. He pulled me forward, locked me in a Shapechanger hold, and started walking faster than I could keep up. Thedar stayed behind, attempting to soothe Spelon's anger.

"If you recall, Shaara, keeping your eyes lowered was one of the items mentioned by Stegthal," Tenor reminded me as we walked. I sighed and studied my stupid lavender slippers for the rest of our walk.

Stegthal had notified Tessa that we were on our way. She greeted us at the door, waving us inside. She'd never been what you'd call a warm, loving person, but this time, she enfolded me in her arms and kissed my cheeks.

"Your pathway has begun, little Shaara. It is a twisted road that will lead you . . ."

"Can you tell when Shaarvan will return? Does the future tell you that?" I interrupted.

"Shaarvan, Shaarvan. Always with you is this obsession. It is not good to focus your life on a male."

Spelon growled, and Tessa turned to glance at him. "I read the future, Tiger lord. Do not interfere. This little one has your destiny in her path— and yours and yours," Tessa said, pointing her finger at each of them. "And there is another . . . not Stegthal, although he will guide her a while and cause her to break away . . . No, that is wrong. He will not be the cause, only the catalyst —— and you, Tiger Lord — you will be another . . . but this other Lord . . . I cannot see him clearly…"

"Tessa, forget him. What about Shaarvan? I don't care about the rest."

Tessa's eyes flared. "Stegthal is right; you *are* a child."

I gasped. I hadn't meant to anger her. I placed my hands in a gesture of contrition.

Tessa was silent a moment, studying me. Her eyes shifted to the others. She gestured for them to sit, not that they needed her permission, but it was a courtesy to do so. Tenor and Thedar both placed themselves on a bench. Only Spelon stood beside us, listening, his brow gathered tightly in a frown.

Tessa's eyes traveled from Spelon, then back to me. I still held my position, hoping I hadn't angered her. She clasped my hands in hers and pushed them down. Her eyes softened, and she raised one wrinkled hand to pat my cheek.

"He will return to you, Shaara of Altar, but only to leave again. What will he give you in trade for your tears?"

"I love him, Tessa."

"And what does he give you for that love? Nothing — but the mentality of a slave girl who . . ."

"She is a wife of High Honors," Thedar called out.

"Be careful what you say to Shaara, woman," Spelon added, growling slightly.

Tessa's eyes grew angry again. "Ah, yes. Shaara is a pretty little plaything to you, Shapechanger."

Thedar bolted from his seat, in half-Shapechange. His hands held claws. Tenor and Spelon both flung themselves on him before he could attack the Old One.

At the sight of his readiness to attack, Tessa began to cackle. The sound rebounded off the walls, all around us, overhead, echoing louder and louder.

I threw my hands over my ears and cried, "Please, Tessa, stop!" The sudden silence awed me. I watched as my bondmates backed towards the door, their hands over their ears, their faces masks of pain.

"Shaara, come," Spelon ordered, seeing I was not at their side.

I meant to obey. I tried to move my feet toward my retreating bondmates, but my toes were granite.

"She will be fine," Tessa called out. "Wait outside."

My bondmates continued to back away, but I could see they were struggling. Their faces were strained with agony. Their calls in my mind ordered me to come. Commanding me to obey. And their eyes — Spelon's, sick with desperation, Thedar's . . . The door slammed shut.

Tessa let out one last wild, high screech and then turned to me. "With Power, my dear, you do not *need* to obey the males. Tell me that you don't want that."

I didn't know how to answer such a thing. I couldn't do what she'd done. Was she mocking me?

Again, she laughed, but this time, I knew she was laughing at me. "Come, you silly child."

My feet, without hesitation, moved me forward.

Spelon, outside the residence of the Head Priestess of Westla

How I despise that Priestess, that old woman, cantankerous as a Psuk. For her to say those things to Shaara! We would never think of Shaara as a play toy. She is a Trendacons, a member of the highest family of Altar, and the mother of a son. We prize her and honor her with our esteem. How dare Tessa accuse us of treating Shaara as a common . . . I cannot say the word in Shaara's proximity. Her ears are too delicate.

But never do we think of Shaara that way. Never.

What shall we tell Stegthal? How could we have allowed a *woman* to chase us from her dwelling? How could we have left Shaara unattended? We have disgraced ourselves. We are not Warlords — we are groundwalkers!

I pace back and forth in front of the door. How many hours will she hold our little Shaara? What shall we do? How can we get back into the dwelling? She has sealed the doors from us. What if she hurts Shaara? Would she do that?

Tenor and Thedar continually halt me. Their faces are ill with frustration. They will not admit their worry, and yet they dare to berate me! I brush my friends aside and continue my movement. I cannot be still. I cannot stop this helpless feeling of unease.

My Shaara, dare I say that? No, I cannot, yet the way I feel racks my body with pain so physical I look for the wound. What did the Priestess mean by saying that I would be a catalyst? Did she mean I would possess Shaara in the future? Was it possible? Would there come a Tide that Shaara would look at me as she did at Shaarvan? Would I feel the warmth of her body beneath mine? Would I own her and fly her to our oneness? If something happened to Stegthal, it would come to that. If Shaarvan had not yet returned, of course.

I could not prevent my thoughts from recalling the pleasantness of Shaara's slender body, the way her breasts peaked and asked for the caress of my hand, the tiny waist that my hand spanned easily, the way her upraised chin dared me to seize her and conquer her . . . I could not think of Shaara that way and still maintain my sanity. I must think of her as my sister, the wife of another. I must hold to that.

Stegthal will be angry over Tessa's actions. He will punish Tessa. But how can a Shapechanger punish a Priestess? Can it be done? I have heard many stories of Priestesses. I think, now, that some of them may be true. I have never known a woman with the kind of Power Tessa showed. Yet, how could I, a Warrior, have retreated from her cackling? She was only a woman. I should have . . .

Thenos, in the Palace on Altar

My informers tell me that Shaarvan landed. My princess was not with him. The unjustness of it! I have been patient, more than patient. How dare my Shaara not be on that ship!

I shall make Shaarvan pay for this wrong. His son shall die, then I shall rip the skin from Shaarvan's chest and dine on his liver. I shall savor the torture of my dear, sweet brother.

Why have they not caught him yet? He was stolen away from me by his followers. How could he have followers? He was gone. Yet, there were soldiers there, soldiers ready to die for him.

When will I see Shaarvan dead? Where is my princess?

Shaara, inside the residence of the Head Priestess of Westla

Stegthal was angry when he came for me.

"How dare you separate Shaara from her bondmates, Old Woman," he roared as he entered.

I wilted in my seat, frightened he would blame me, but his eyes scarcely noticed me after his first Warrior's scan. He faced Tessa in full stance. I prayed to Barquel that I would not be pulled into whatever occurred as Stegthal and Tessa came to battle.

Tessa laughed, her posture showing no fear of Stegthal. "Her bondmates irritated me, old man," was Tessa's careless reply.

If this were a catfight, the fur would already be flying, or so I thought. But Stegthal only glared at her a moment and then suddenly relaxed and joined her laughter. He walked closer to Tessa and then kissed her on each cheek.

"Come for your plaything, huh?" Tessa asked him, kissing him back — on the mouth.

"Do not start that with me, woman. I would be happy to remind you of the Power of the Shapechanger male." Stegthal said, but I saw he was no longer angry. In fact, he was flirting with Tessa.

"Promises promises," she cackled and backed away.

Stegthal then turned to view me. "Come here, Shaara," Stegthal ordered. My feet obliged, and Stegthal's arm wrapped me in the Shapechanger hold.

"She will never be yours, Stegthal," Tessa told him, her hand reaching out to touch his sleeve.

"I know. I am not a young, besotted fool," he agreed, and once again, his voice was laden with irritation.

He steered me towards the outer door and then stopped and looked back at Tessa. "Shaara will return tomorrow. She is to be given instruction on temperance and control, not how to revenge herself on males. Do we agree on that?"

Tessa paused. Her eyes roamed Stegthal's body. "It would be almost worth it to be ridden by you, High Lord," she said, then sighed. "But, agreed. I will tutor the child in temperance and control."

Stegthal raised an eyebrow. "Let me know if you change your mind, Tessa. I would look forward to it. And try to be kinder to Shaara's keepers, old woman."

Tessa didn't answer, but she grinned.

My bondmates pooled about us as we came out through the door. "You are well?" Spelon demanded. "She did not harm you?"

I didn't have a chance to assure him.

"Ease your mind, Spelon. Tessa would never hurt Shaara, but she enjoys taunting males."

The males laughed rather nervously, I thought.

Stegthal moved us forward, and the conversation flowed with good-hearted spirits. Since Stegthal had accepted Tessa's behavior, the males accepted the earlier lapse of what they deemed their rights and moved on, but we had taken no more than ten steps away from Tessa's portal when the Priestess came running out. "There is danger," she said.

Stegthal wheeled us about. I suspected my ribcage would have new bruises.

"What kind of danger, Tessa? To whom?"

"To the baby. Do not leave the son of Shaarvan at the nursery. Keep him with you, always."

"Shaarac? My baby?" I cried.

Stegthal's hand slid over my mouth. "Silence," he whispered. He nodded formally to Tessa. "We are grateful, High Priestess. Is there more?"

She shook her head. Her eyes darted to me. "Guard her well, Shapechanger. This little one, Shaara, is important to us all. She will . . . I can tell you no more but protect her well."

I thought Stegthal would take affront to Tessa's words, but he didn't. "We shall heed your warnings, High Priestess. You have our Saberey gratitude. "

Tessa turned and retreated back into her dwelling. Stegthal watched her a second, then called out to the others. "Thedar, you and Tenor go get Shaarac and hurry. Spelon, you stay with us and be on guard. Shaara's safety may rest on our skills."

Only then did Stegthal move his hand from my mouth. "Listen to me, Shaara. You must be quiet." He laid the silence command on my lips as if his words had not been enough. "Everything will be fine. Your bondmates will take care of Shaarac. You are not to worry."

He seemed to expect me to respond in some way, but he'd ordered me not to speak. I nodded.

"Good girl. You know Spelon is the best Warrior on Westla. You will be safe with us, but he and I depend on you not to distract our concentration. Promise me."

I nodded again. I wasn't worried about *my* safety. I had confidence in them. Besides, hadn't Tessa prophesied that the danger was for Shaarac?

Our passage home was without incident. Shaarvan played the Warrior well, and I could feel the tense readiness in Stegthal. I remembered the ruffians who'd attacked us on Altar. They'd thrown a stun net over me and wounded Shaarvan.

The next time, they'd succeeded despite heavy guards, almost killing Shaarvan and tossing me into slavehood. There were indeed many threats to women, and I was grateful for Spelon and Stegthal's protection, but it was Shaarac I worried about. My baby was the one who Tessa claimed was under threat.

I walked faster than I'd ever walked before, praying that my son would be there before us. And he was, safe and content, playing happily in the entertainment room with Tenor and Thedar. I sank to the floor to kiss and hug him. Then I smiled at my bondmates.

"Thank you," I said.

Stegthal, in his residence on Westla

I sent word to Tem concerning Tessa's foretelling. The First came for a visit in the afternoon. He gave Shaara his greeting and looked her over superficially. Then he used his Power on her, a fact that neither she nor I liked, but it was only a brief scan. I reminded myself that not only is Tem Westla's First but also the girl's uncle. As head of the Trendacons on Westla, I suppose it was his duty to check on her occasionally.

When Tem was finished with Shaara, I sent the child to her work space. She still had trigonometry to complete and had yet to begin her newest sequences. I am a firm believer that math improves thinking skills and helps to learn temperance.

I formed two soft-seated chairs over to the side so Tem and I could talk comfortably. That way, I could still keep on eye on Shaara's activities while finding out what Tem had stopped by to say.

He thanked me for my good care of Shaara, which I could have seen as an insult since, of course, as her new husband, it was my duty to treat her well, but I chose to view it as merely the opening for further conversation.

Next Tem thanked me for letting him know of Tessa's latest premonition. I imagine the Priestess also acquainted Tem about the threat to Shaarac, so I doubted my note was overly beneficial.

But courtesies rendered, the meat of his visit finally arrived. Either he wished to use me as a sounding board, or he was warning me that we must all be on higher alert.

Speaking in *Nezten*, the male language of the Shapechanger, Tem gave me background, filling in details of the events on Altar. Thenos labeled *the mad one* by Tem, was killing indiscriminately. According to Westlan spies, *the mad one* was using daily doses of Power enhancers, engaging in long dialogues with himself, and constantly issuing orders that he reversed almost immediately. Most of the Commoners were cowed by the force of his Power, which was so unbalanced it formed a dizzying wake around him.

Frightened by that and by his bizarre behavior and speech, the servants did their best to provide for his every desire. Smarter Commoners, who kept their distance from this erratic new leader, used *the mad one* as a unifying banner in their long-cherished effort to finally get rid of the Shapechanger.

"But how can a Commoner stand up to a Shapechanger Warrior?" I asked

Tem sighed with the heaviness of long bouts of exasperation. "Only 2% of Altarians are Shapechanger Warriors. Most are statesmen, researchers, and traders like the Trendacons, although, of course, *her* husband, as you know, is fully trained."

I was pleased Tem refrained from using names. I did not want Shaara to be further upset. If she knew we were discussing Shaarvan, she'd be insisting on information.

Shaara suddenly stood up, glanced our way, and then scurried off to the necessary room. She always seemed apologetic about it, as if she thought I'd mind any stoppage of her work. Surely I was not that severe a task master.

"The Commoners have weapons that *the mad one* imported," Tem said. "The Shapechanger have only their Powers. Many of them still refuse to see what is happening. They think the Commoners will kill *the mad one*, and then everything will continue as before. But that is most unlikely."

Tem issued another heavy sigh and said, "The Westlan troops are leaving tomorrow. Five ships have been readied. When they make landfall, they will join the opposition."

"And your nephew?" I asked, referring to Shaarvan obliquely since Shaara was back at her table, working on sequences.

"He has joined the rebellion, of course. I believe they have made him their war leader."

So, war was the reality, just as Shaarvan had suspected. And as Shaarvan had foretold, he would be in the thick of it.

Chapter Five

Shaara, on the artificial planet, Westla

How quickly people adapt to change. A twentyTide ago, Stegthal had been a stranger to me, yet, now, he seemed like he'd always been a part of my life. I'd even started calling his dwelling "home," and it had begun to seem like it was. All the odd, little habits and patterns of Stegthal were becoming familiar. Thus does an interlude become your realm, and you forget what the Wheel teaches . . . that life is a rushing river heading for the falls.

I thought that all around me lay security and stability, but inside me, the wild tiger was growing. During the Tides, Tessa drilled me so hard I could scarcely feel its pressure. And at home, I pored through the books that Stegthal had purchased for me. I played with Shaarac. But at night, I couldn't sleep.

In bed, Stegthal held me in his arms, and I would wait for his soft, gentle breathing to tell me he slumbered. Then, I would get out of bed and pace throughout the night. I think Stegthal suspected. His eyes grew haunted. One night, he came for me.

"You must come back to bed," he ordered, and his arms swallowed me, pressing me back against him.

"But I can't sleep."

"That is my fault, my dear," Stegthal said as he brushed back my hair and touched his lips to my forehead. "You are burning yourself up with it. Your Power is strong, but you cannot hold out much longer."

I darted a glance at his face. "I'm fine, Stegthal. I'm just not tired."

His hand continued to caress my cheek. The touch of his fingers on my face was an irritant. I wanted to bat his hand away and snarl with rage at his touch.

"I had hoped, Shaara, that you would grow used to me. But still, you reject my touch."

There was nothing I could say to that. He knew my thoughts. My fingers itched to grow claws.

He lifted me and carried me back to the bed. The quilt was cold. Stegthal covered me with his arms. His lips kissed my cheek. I lay still and waited for him to stop. How long would it take for Stegthal to fall asleep this time? How long would I be forced to lie beside him, strangled by heavy, foreign arms? I sighed and ached to be free.

But Stegthal didn't stop as he usually did. His mouth moved to nibble at my neck. His body felt hot against my skin. Then his fingers began to sketch patterns on my body, and I realized he was weaving the Shapechanger web.

I bolted away, growling. "Stop it, Stegthal. Don't touch me."

His arms restrained me and pulled me back. "No, Shaara. You are a breath away from Change. I must take you now."

"I can't, Stegthal. Please don't..."

"I am your husband. You will obey."

I lashed out at him with my knee. He swore in a foreign tongue. "I am not your enemy," he rasped between gritted teeth.

His hands buckled my wrists. I bit the closer arm.

"Foolish child," he scolded, and he flipped me over like a half-done pancake. The sting of his hand against my naked skin made my rage snarl. I writhed, my claws scratching him more than once, but his heavy hand came pounding down on my rear. Five times.

He stopped, then turned me over. "You will accept the web and my possession of you, Wife."

I shook my head. Once more, I felt the urge to Change, but his hand was already roaming my skin, building a Shapechanger web. My teeth sank into his skin when his hand touched my face. He slapped me, but he didn't pause otherwise. When he freed my wrists, believing I was strapped in tightly, my claws scratched rivulets into his skin. Then he webbed my hands.

"I do not want to hurt you, Shaara," Stegthal attempted to soothe me. "Do not continue this mindless struggle."

"Then don't rape me, Stegthal," I screamed.

"Foolish girl."

"I belong to Shaarvan."

He didn't respond, but his fingers continued their design, and the web snapped into completion. Then, I could only lie there, hating Stegthal.

His body was sized the same as Shaarvan's — his arms as heavily muscled, his belly just as flat, but there were no dimples in his smiles, no pelt of fine, soft golden-brown hair, no eyes that were soft and loving. Others might have found Stegthal handsome, but he was not Shaarvan, and I was repelled.

"Your precious Shaarvan . . . is that all that brain of yours contains? I shall show you that life continues, even without Shaarvan."

He wove me deeper in Shapechanger magic. I had never felt such a force. The Power in it made me dizzy. My body felt disconnected. Stegthal's fingers teased and beckoned until it was suddenly *my* mind I was struggling against.

He laughed. "There are pleasures you have never known, my dear. I have toured the galaxies looking for them."

I could not fight what he was doing. All I had was my mind. When Stegthal played another tune to weave me tighter, I shouted out, "Shaarvan."

He slapped me, but I laughed because I had felt a web snap. He redid the pattern, but when I shouted "Shaarvan" the second time, Stegthal's Power twisted the word, and it came out "Stegthal."

He thrust into me then, the victor. He thoroughly played the knight with sword. My body felt all the wondrous sensations Stegthal's sword and hands could bring. And when he brought me to the heights, I felt the bonding chord between us tighten. Then, after it was over. Stegthal released me from the web and rolled over onto his side.

I had no time to speak the words that seethed inside me. I felt sick. Waves of nausea assaulted me. Before I could move, I vomited over the side of the bed. I heaved until I was empty and lay gasping for air. The smell of my vomit sickened me, and I gagged and suffered dry heaves.

Throughout it, Stegthal's hand insultingly patted my back. I was embarrassed, hurt, and furious. Yet, I couldn't move away from him. My stomach ached, and my head was twirling the path of a children's top.

"It is all right, Shaara. You will feel better in a moment. It is the bond reforming inside you that brings this illness. It only happens the first time. It will be easier next time."

"Next time, I will kill you." Waves of nausea attacked a second time. My body attempted to vomit, but there was nothing left inside me.

"If you are through feeling sorry for yourself, reverse what you just said."

Again, I heaved, my stomach practically twisting itself inside out. Pain. Nausea. It hurt so much. Tears ran down my cheeks.

"I will not kill you," I sobbed. Immediately, as I reversed the lie, the nausea subsided. I hated Stegthal even more for being right.

When I lasted a minute without vomiting, Stegthal picked me up and carried me to the bathroom. I was limp as an overused pillow and no longer cared what he did to me.

Inside the water, Stegthal held me in his arms, spraying us both. At one point, I filled my mouth and spit out the vile taste. Otherwise, I lay in his arms like a dead animal, saying nothing, desiring nothing, and feeling empty inside.

Stegthal took me through the drier exit, then returned me to the bed. The cleaner robot had already scurried out and sucked up all the mess, then soaped and dried the carpet. The room once again smelled sweet. Even the bed had been remade with clean sheets. It was like none of it had happened, except that my body ached all over, and I felt different.

Stegthal sat down beside me. His hand brushed back my hair. His eyes softened. They were almost blue-gray as he stared down at me.

"Why? Why did you have to do that?" I cried.

His hand continued to stroke my hair as his eyes watched me. "Shaarvan told me that I would have to take you against your will. I did not like the forcing of you, Shaara. I wish you could have desired me."

I shuddered. He pulled a blanket up over my body. "I have wanted you since the Tide I bonded you . . . " he said.

Again, I turned my head away.

"To touch you inside where my fingers knew you, to feel your lips on mine. I wanted you to feel that need, too . . ."

"I will never. . ." I said, still looking away.

His finger covered my lips in the Shapechanger command for silence. "I wanted to see the Tide when you no longer cringed at my touch."

I wished I dared tell him how much I despised him.

"You may hate me for a while, my wife, but your body knows its master. You will soon welcome me to your nights."

That was more than I could handle. "I will never welcome you. I will fight you every time you take me, and I shall spend my Tides cursing you."

"I should beat you for disobeying Shapechanger command," Stegthal said, "but I think there is a better way to discipline the wildness in you. I shall keep you hostage in this room until your temper cools and you are ready to obey."

He rose then and left me. I didn't miss him. I fell asleep, scheming how I could get even.

I awakened later when Stegthal brought in Shaarac. The baby was dry and clean and had already been fed. I would have thanked Stegthal, but I was still so angry my body felt fat with it. I vowed never to speak to Stegthal again.

He read my thoughts and laughed, then left. I dressed and played with Shaarac. My son was easy to entertain, always willing to be lifted up or gently tossed. He loved to crawl around the floor, and his strong, little arms worked at pulling his body up. He could walk several steps, and he loved to practice with me holding his hands.

But that Tide, it was my slippers that entertained him. He wore them on his feet, hands, and head. He giggled and chortled, then tossed them up into the air. I showed him how to play catch, but he wasn't good at it. He preferred peek-a-boo much better.

While he was scooting a slipper around the room, I tested the bedroom door to see if the current was on. I was not locked in, but Stegthal's command was enough to keep me inside. Besides, why would I want to leave my sanctuary? I didn't have to look at Stegthal inside *this* room.

Later, Thedar came in. He glowered at me, and I realized he'd been told I was in trouble. Why did a male always assume the female was in the wrong? Why did Thedar not ask for my side?

My bondmate didn't speak. He went directly to Shaarac and picked him up.

To my surprise, I broke into tears. "Please don't take him away from me," I pleaded, laying my hand on Thedar's arm.

"Your mommy's fine, Shaarac, just spoiled and stubborn," Thedar said when Shaarac's face crinkled up, tears about to burst.

I realized, then, that Thedar wasn't speaking to me. Had Stegthal forbidden it, or was my bondmate punishing me, too?

"Your mommy will be better tomorrow," Thedar said, removing my hand from his arm. Without looking at me, he turned and walked out through the door.

I cried for a long time, sobbing over what Stegthal had done to me and over everything that had happened to me since the Shapechanger captured me. And then, I wept because Shaarvan was still gone.

It must have been hours later when Stegthal entered.

"Come here, Shaara," he ordered.

I rose but took only a step or two before stopping.

Stegthal shook his head. "Your belly growls from lack of food. You are alone and desolate. I am your husband, the one who will feed you and comfort you. I shall take care of your every need, my little one. Come."

I shook my head, but Shapechanger magic was flowing all around me. Stegthal was weaving a web from clear across the room. How could that be possible?

"You do not yet know my Power, Wife. I am strong, stronger than most Shapechanger. It is knowledge that gives me strength. I have traveled a lifetime, more Passes than you have even known. I have spent all that time collecting secrets."

Stegthal was confusing me. The questions burst from my mind, running down my tongue and spinning into the air. I forgot I'd meant to stay silent. "How could you have traveled that long? You're no older than Shaarvan. Where have you gone? What secrets?"

He stepped closer, smiling down at me. "Would you like to hear of my travels, Shaara? I have viewed the aliens you are curious about. They are vivid in my mind. I have seen a hundred civilizations spread across galaxies from planets you have never heard of."

He had captured my mind so completely I was unaware of his webbing. When his hands lifted to stroke my hair, I couldn't move to pull away.

"I have collected all those secrets, Shaara. Would you like to see them?"

How had his lips found my neck? I groaned when he nipped me.

"They are in a book, Shaara." His hands were lifting up my dress. I wanted to stop him, but my limbs were puppet's legs in a master's hands.

How had we reached the bed? I couldn't remember. His lips on my face were circling. It wasn't a Shapechanger pattern. What was he doing?

"There are many secrets in alien hands, my dear."

His lips on my breasts were pulling me away from my body. I was there on the bed, and yet I was up above, watching.

His hands slid over my belly. Why did I lie there? Why didn't I arch at the feel of his hands?

His lips were on mine. His tongue played. The taste of him was intoxicating, yet I couldn't touch him. I couldn't move from the heights where I watched.

"Come back, little Shaara. It is time. Join us. You have seen how easy it is now."

I was me again, back in my body, and the feel of his hands touching and petting my skin made me wild.

"Yes. Feel me. Know me."

He drove into me then, and I could not stop the wildness. All the energy bottled by my anger soared outward to a higher pitch. We rode it together. And in concert, we came in a burst of dazzling fire.

"Oh, Shaara," Stegthal said, rolling off me. "You are a wild ride. I had forgotten how good a Shapechanger woman felt in the throes of ecstasy. You were worth the wait."

He lay by my side. I felt his breathing warm and slightly fast against my neck, but it was his eyes watching me that disturbed me. There was something wrong.

I felt no nausea the second time. Stegthal had been right, but there was also a blackness, a despair that hurt. I tried to think of landoors or astronomy or anything but the agony I was feeling. The tears, always eager to shed my life force, slowly dribbled down onto the bed. Stegthal said nothing, but his eyes watched, and I felt the tendrils of his mind inside mine.

Thenos, in the Palace on Altar

It has been a QuarterPass of worry and wonder. I have scarcely eaten. I have not enjoyed the pleasure of my whores. I have paced the floors of the halls and palace.

Finally my spies have discovered that Shaara is still on Westla with Shaarvan's child. I should have known Shaarvan would leave her there. Of all places for her to be! I cannot steal her from Westla. She is too well protected. Curse the stars. Curse the Somber Tree.

As if that were not bad enough, Shaarvan has given her a Second. Another Shapechanger is touching her. Another is placing his hands on her soft, tender body. I grind my teeth in despair. I cannot endure this torture.

My rage needs vent, but still, they have not captured my brother. Fools. My troops are all dirtwalkers. How I cringe at their incompetence. How difficult can it be to kill Shaarvan?

My heart races when I become angry. I must not hold onto my fury. I shall capture Shaarvan. I shall. I shall. And then the sweetness of my Shaara will be mine. I shall take her as my wife, whether she likes it or not. She will learn. And, I shall enjoy the teaching of her. Her eyes will snap at me for a while, but I shall caress her softness. I shall nip at her delicate neck. I shall tune her body to mine.

I journeyed to my princess yesterTide. The seed of the *Nipa-seed* took me to her side. I tapped her dreams. I saw her naked and trembling before me. The delight of it almost eased the agony of our separation. Almost, I could touch her. Almost, I could place my lips on hers.

She did not know me. She thought she was dreaming of her home world. I allowed her to think that. I do not wish her to be frightened. She is so innocent.

I have called her to me, but she is weak. She is only a girl. I cannot expect her to be strong enough to come here. Yet, my call will familiarize her with the feel of me.

I have built the web of this dream world between us. The lines are formed. It will be easier to go to her next time. I shall play with her many nights, but always, I shall keep my identity secret. Each morning, she will not remember. I must do it this way. I do not want her new Lord to discover what I am about.

Ah, my sweet, sweet princess, you will soon be mine. The dream world is not enough. I shall find a way to steal you away. Not even Westla can keep you from me, my princess.

Shaara, on the artificial planet, Westla

I was attempting to eat a meal when my bondmates came back with Shaarac. I hugged and kissed my son, but he belonged to a different plane. My bondmates would take care of him.

I can feel the snow piling up all around me. It is not cold yet, but it will be soon. I welcomed the snow once when Shaarvan led me to it. I hadn't known I loved him then, and his cruelty drove me to it.

Teea and Tevor, Shaarvan's parents, stopped me. But they are not here now, and my bondmates will not know that I can choose the snow.

I put down the meal Stegthal served me. I have no desire to eat. Shaarvan has left me. My bondmates have told me why, but I can't remember. It is not important. The snow will not leave me. It will stay with me forever.

"Shaara, stop it," Stegthal commands me sharply.

I look at him for an instant, but he has no meaning. The snow, piling all around me, is white and lovely. It offers me a soft, pillowed bed.

"Get Tessa, quickly!" Stegthal yells at the others.

For a moment, I look at him, wondering why he yells. He is a Shapechanger. They do not yell. They are coldly angry . . . fierce, but icy quiet.

"Shaara, stand up and walk with me," Stegthal orders.

"I am too tired," I tell him, but he forces me. I sag against him. "Please let me lie down. I am sleepy."

"You are not. Wake up."

His legs move too fast for me. I want to watch the snow falling. Like lacy white doilies, it decorates the floors and carpeting. The meal I started to eat is covered in it. The beauty of the crystals draws my eyes.

"It is six-sided, you know," I tell Stegthal.

"No, Shaara, that is wrong. Perhaps there are seven sides. Count them."

"One, two, three, four . . . no, you are mistaken. I see them. There are six."

Stegthal is shaking his head at me. "No, Shaara. See the one over there?"

I look at Stegthal's finger. It is white with frost. He makes a handsome snowman.

"Shaara, walk with me. I command you."

"Silly man. Snowmen can't walk."

"You are right," he says, dragging me along faster. "We shall run. Run with me, Shaara."

Stegthal yanks me across the carpet. It is hard to run through the piles of snow.

"I am exhausted," I say. "Let me rest."

Stegthal does not allow me to stop. The snow is warm and friendly. It offers company. Why does Stegthal not let me join with it? He pushes me on and on.

For a long time, he makes me walk-jog, and his sharp voice keeps piercing my calm. His body forces me to move. Can he not hear the voice of the snow? It calls to me. It offers quiet and friendship.

"I am weary. Please let me stop," I beg, but he will not listen.

"Weary, my foot. You coward!" says a jarring voice. I know that voice, but I can't focus on it.

"Snap out of it, girl! I didn't do all that work training you for you to take such an easy road!" Tessa yells.

Why is Tessa here? Why is everyone yelling? The snow is hushed. Can they not feel the magic of it?

"Drink this, Shaara," Tessa orders, shoving a vial of foul-smelling liquid under my nose. I don't want to open my mouth, but Tenor and Stegthal force it down my throat.

It burns. I scream. My screaming drives the snow away — my quiet, peaceful snow. All around me, I see it melting, disappearing, rejecting me, leaving me behind to face the pain.

"What drove her to it?" Tessa demands angrily.

"I took possession of her," Stegthal says.

Why are they talking all around me? Can't they see the snow is deserting me? Without it I will be forced to remain on *their* plane of existence. Can't they see that something's wrong?

"You fool! Could you not have given her more time?" Tessa growled. She strides toward me and wraps her arms around me. I don't flinch or try to move away. What does anything matter when the snow has denied me?

Tessa leads me a short distance. She sits me down and pulls me into her lap. I do not like the feel of her arms about me, but I say nothing. My eyes are searching for even one stray patch of snow.

I feel the thrust of Tessa's mind burning into mine. I whimper and instinctively attempt to flee, but I am caught. Her touch is not as gentle as Stegthal's. My head begins to pound, and tears flow down my cheeks.

"Stegthal, you will have to seed her," Tessa tells him. "She is too close to the edge. It is the only way to keep her from choosing death again."

Tessa's hands are gently stroking my hair. I want to tell her that her hands are scorching me. They burn right through my skull. I whisper, "Too hot." But she doesn't listen.

"Do it now, Stegthal, do it while she is still in shock." Tessa's hands pull back my hair, and she stares into my face. "Do not wait another moment, Stegthal. She is icy cold. Take her now."

Stegthal lifts me up out of Tessa's lap. His hands blister my skin, too. I moan. "Too hot. Too hot."

Like Tessa, Stegthal ignores me. His body is a furnace against my skin as he carries me to the bedroom. His hands are flying across my body. I recognize the patterns.

"Shaarvan, you don't need to web me," I tell him. "I will always be yours."

He doesn't answer. His hands continue to stroke me.

"Do not hurry so, Shaarvan. We have time."

But Shaarvan is in such a hurry. He takes me before I am ready. The pain of it is unbelievable. I cry out.

"Shaarvan," I protest when he is finished. "That wasn't like you. Why did you hurt me?"

He still doesn't speak. His arms hold me bolted to his body. I do not protest. It is right for Shaarvan to hold me so. I close my eyes and listen to the strength of his heartbeat. The melody carries me into sleep.

Tren

When I woke up, my head ached, and my throat was parched. I could scarcely swallow. I knew I was ill and obviously in a hospital ward. A Shapechanger in a long gray robe was on guard. He noticed my open eyes. He walked over and ordered me to drink from a straw he inserted into my mouth.

I sipped, but the water dribbled down my neck. I could not swallow. He left me and returned in a moment with a needler. He plunged it down into my arm. Whatever he gave me, it burned. I closed my eyes and waited for the agony to pass.

After the shot, I found I was able to drink, but my throat was still so parched I couldn't speak. I lay there for hours, breathing in the scent of bananas and uncut wheat. No one came to see me. At intervals, the same gray-robed Shapechanger ordered me to sip from the tube.

Much later, Targone visited. He told me the captain had left and informed me I had been sleeping for many Tides. Targone rattled on about research he was working on. They'd allowed him to enroll in the university, and he was ecstatic about his progress. He gave me no time to ask him questions. I fell asleep listening to him talk.

I think it was the next Tide when Tem first visited. It was he who explained I had been given the Shapechanger DNA.

"My choice?" I croaked out.

He shook his head. "You should have been born Shapechanger, Tren. We only corrected a mistake."

I wondered what had happened to my decision in the matter. Did they not believe in free choice? Was this how they rewarded service to their race?

"Soon, you will realize how fortunate you are. You are now a Lord on your little planet, Freinana, and you are an heir to the fortune of the Trendacons — a high and esteemed Shapechanger family. In addition, you are now legally my nephew. Why should you regret what has been done?

"We shall test you when you are able. I am sure you will rate high. Perhaps you will become a Warlord. That would make you esteemed among all Shapechanger.

"And eventually, you will meet your family. We shall reunite you with Shaarvan and his wife — your sister now. You have cause *only for celebration*. Welcome to Westla."

My voice allowed few words. What could I have said anyway? It was too late. What they had done could not be undone.

I had slept through most of my transition. My recovery was swift. Soon, I was bathed and given Westlan attire. And in the Tides that followed, allowed to sit up. And then, my training began.

Unknown Shapechanger filtered into my room bringing me a flower, a book, or an invitation to their favorite sport or hobby for later when I was fully recovered. These strangers smiled at me and welcomed me to Westla. Their minds were open to my scrutiny, their hands ready to touch me in a pledge of friendship.

The pretty girl who served me the meal at Tem's came almost daily to bring me delicacies. She crawled into my bed on her second visit. I was surprised when she showed me things I hadn't known.

I learned from her, from my visitors, and from the Old Ones who had begun to engage me in an *expansion of my knowledge*, as they put it. I also found out why Targone and Jorvanel had been so free with their information. They had known that I would be forced into transition. To them, I had already been a Shapechanger.

I suppose I should be furious with Westla and the Shapechanger. I should remind them of the rights of citizens and all that, but what good would it do? When the die is cast, it's too late to ponder whether one should have wagered.

Besides, I was still missing my little landoor girl. Whether she was the wife of an elite or not, I wanted to find her. I needed to know she was all right. Being Shapechanger — Shaarvan's brother yet — was the only way that Shapechanger would permit me to be near her. Of course, I wasn't overly pleased at being Shaara's brother, but I never had a chance at being more. She had already been owned. Less would have to do.

Note: Wow! I just had a birds and the bees dialogue with Tem, my new uncle, and head of Westla. He informed me that Shapechanger have no fear of venereal diseases (or any other diseases) and that there are no pregnancy worries with a nonShapechanger since our species are no longer co-viable.

Tem also informed me that intercourse with the Priestesses, if we mutually choose, is never a danger in terms of pregnancy. In fact, apparently, I must *turn on* my desire to plant a child. (What an interesting concept.) Tem added that the success of intentional procreation is 100% successful in a single discharge and unquestionable since the enhanced sperm attach with a sharp stab of pain felt by both parties.

That conversation, one of many over a variety of subjects, was the most embarrassing. I have to admit that I sometimes felt as if I'd entered the kingdom of weird.

Thenos, in the Palace on Altar

Curse the Soaring Eagle; Shaarvan still escapes me. It is only for the moment. The rebels aid him. I am sure of that. I shall strike at them and punish Shaarvan for his duplicity.

I have the perfect weapon at my disposal now. I have finally gotten one of my mercenaries into Westla. Chaslow is a Shapechanger from Despega whose grievance with the League throws him into allegiance with me, and I bless his vindictive nature.

Shaara would not blame me if her husband deserted her and allowed their son to be killed. Shaarvan should have been there at her side. That is the job of a husband. Yet Shaarvan left her, and the poor girl will soon be defenseless.

I smile with satisfaction at my cunning. Chaslow will destroy Shaara's Second, end the problem of an unwanted child, and then bring my princess to me.

The only wrinkle is the thought of Shaara alone on that ship with Chaslow. She would quickly go into Shapechanger heat. Thus, I have told him to put her into deep sleep. It is best. It will not hurt her, and even better, she will be ripe for me.

It is a shame Chaslow is not a lover of men, but he is not. I have supplied him with a blonde I am tired of. I cannot remember her name.

It is unimportant, except that she will keep Chaslow's lust away from my princess. (I train my whores well. She will be grateful for an easier rider.)

Soon, Chaslow will bring my Shaara to me. Her crown is ready. It has blue and red stones — sapphires and rubies. I think she will like the pattern, and there are diamonds running across the bottom. It will shine like her eyes when the sunlight streams in. I hope it is not too heavy for her. She has a small, dainty head and a tiny neck. I remember well how small it was. One hand could reach almost twice around her neck.

I have had a ceremonial robe created for her, in white, of course, but red and blue stones have been sewn across the top to match her crown. I can imagine Shaara sitting there beside me on her throne. She will raise her eyes to me, and I shall see her smile. She has such an innocent smile, so full of sweetness and purity.

I wonder if her breasts will show through the material of her dress. Should I permit that? Shaara's breasts are very white. I remember the first time I saw them through the gown Shaarvan had forced her to wear. She was embarrassed when she saw my eyes on her. I loved the way she blushed and covered herself. I do not like the thought of prying eyes on my princess, but the delicate pink of her nipples would look enchanting through the fabric.

What would it be like to suck her breasts through that soft, silky cloth? Soon, I shall know.

Do not fail me, Chaslow. Bring me my princess, and let her be chaste. If you dare to touch her, you will know the Power of the Trendacons and *beware*. The Elders of Despega know little of revenge, but I am an expert!

Shaara, on the artificial planet, Westla

The next morning, I woke from the loveliest dream. Shaarvan had made love to me, and he was back. I stretched happily.

A noise from the room beyond made my mind click into focus. Shaarac's high-pitched laugh rents the air. Ah, Shaarvan is playing with his son. But stray thoughts kept nibbling at my mind. Why was I not in *our* chamber then? Why was I still in Stegthal's? I studied the lavender wreath hanging on the wall. On the right was Stegthal's crest, although it held the sacred Saberey, it also had small flower impressions in the metal. Lavender.

Perhaps, Shaarvan's residence was gone. Maybe he'd needed to spend the night here in Stegthal's dwelling? But, it was puzzling. I listened for a while to the noises outside my door and tried to make sense of the pieces. I remembered our joining in the night. Shaarvan had webbed me and then taken me, but it had stung. That didn't make sense. How could I have not been ready for Shaarvan? My husband had only to look at me, and I melted to him.

I wiggled but felt no pain. Isandor had made me sore at times, but I didn't feel like I'd been raped. (Not that Shaarvan would ever do that.) I felt fuzzy, different. Something was wrong, but what?

Why did I not remember Shaarvan's arrival? Tessa had been in the dining room/kitchen, and my bondmates were gathered around me, but I hadn't seen Shaarvan. Everyone had been worried about me. I remembered that. Tessa had made the snow go away, and she'd ordered us to leave Westla. I could recall no more.

I dressed slowly, still confused. The pieces were beginning to assemble on their own. I was no longer sure Shaarvan was back. Why had I thought he was? Had my night dreams been more real than reality?

It was with fresh sadness that I walked into the eating room and discovered boxes stacked up high. Almost every table and chair was filled with books or boxes. Tenor and Spelon were busy carting them off. They nodded to me as they paused before the doorway, their worried eyes searching mine.

Thedar had Shaarac perched on his knee, jiggling him up and down. My son let out a piercing scream and held his arms out for me to pick him up. Happy to do so, I gave him a hug, a kiss, and a tickle. He laughed. His voice was so gleeful I giggled with him. The bondmates stopped and stared as if frozen in a tableau.

"What are you doing with all the boxes?" I asked.

"Do not stop to talk with Shaara," Stegthal barked at everyone. He had only just entered the room, but his presence unfroze the others.

"We must leave within the hour, and there is still much to load," Stegthal lectured them sharply.

Spelon and Tenor exited the room, carrying the heavy boxes they'd been holding. Thedar, freed from his role of babysitter, grabbed a box, and followed after. I was left staring at Stegthal.

Memories stirred. It had been Stegthal's eyes I'd seen in the night — not Shaarvan's. Why had I been confused? Had Stegthal taken me again? He turned away and headed back to his office.

Carrying Shaarac, I followed Stegthal him. "What is happening? Why are there boxes everywhere?"

He stopped and turned. His eyes were hard, and the high arch of his jaw line looked sharp with irritation. "I have no time for childish questions, Shaara, nor for temper tantrums."

I gasped. What had I done to deserve that? I dropped my eyes and started to retreat.

Stegthal sighed. "That was unfair, Shaara. Forgive me." He turned back and began placing books into an opened box.

I was confused. Should I withdraw, or was it safe to ask a question?

Stegthal looked up again, eyeing me strangely. I had been bouncing Shaarac up and down to keep him happy, but my eyes watched Stegthal.

He put a load of books into the box and then walked towards me. When he reached my side, he took Shaarac and placed him on the ground where he could crawl about. Then Stegthal drew me into his arms and kissed my cheek.

"Shaara," he said. "You were in shock last night. I doubt you remember hearing that Thenos has tracked you down. His spies are here, all around us. We must leave Westla and go into hiding."

"Leave? But I can't. Shaarvan won't know where to find me."

"We have no choice. You and Shaarac are in danger. Can you not understand that?"

I shook my head and felt Stegthal's probe. He didn't linger. He dropped his arms and turned away. Then, he walked back to his box and began packing more of his precious books.

"I shall discuss it with you no further, Shaara," he told me without looking up. "I am your husband, and you will obey. We leave within the half."

"Stegthal, please . . ."

He answered me with the *no argument sign.* "Go back to the eating room, Shaara. Eat something, sit down in the chair, and do not move from it."

Shaarac had just immersed himself in a pile of papers and was happily tossing them about. I left the papers scattered, scooped up my son, and carried him away despite his screams. But when I reached the doorway, I stopped and turned.

"Even if you beat me, Stegthal, I am Shaarvan's. I shall wait for him on Westla."

In the eating room, I sat down as ordered and began to think over everything I'd said. When Stegthal finished packing, he would probably beat me. It didn't matter. All that was important was Shaarvan. What would my husband want me to do?

I knew the others would side with Stegthal. They always did. They'd probably take me to the ship, either drugged or screaming and kicking. But if we left, how would Shaarvan find me? Was there a way to notify him of our new location? Would they do so?

Shaarvan had ordered me to obey Stegthal, but had he truly intended for Stegthal to bed me? Had Shaarvan meant for me to belong to another? If so, Shaarvan must be tired of me. Maybe I'd become a hindrance. Perhaps my love had weighed him down. Had the words he'd said to me only been Shapechanger lies that I didn't have the power to see through?

Everyone kept telling me that Shaarvan had given me to Stegthal to protect Shaarac and myself, but they didn't know Shaarvan well. They hadn't observed his jealousness when men danced with me and touched my hand. They hadn't seen the possessiveness of his grip when other eyes wanted me or Shaarvan's rage at Thenos' words.

Had I lost Shaarvan when he found out I'd been with another on Freinana? Had Isandor's lust killed my husband's love? Shaarvan told me it hadn't, but maybe the memories had come to him in the night and had slowly eaten away his desire. How could he tell me his heart beat the words "Shaara, Shaara" — and then hand me to another?

I needed so badly to talk with him! Even if he no longer wanted me, I would crawl to him. Let him take me as his slave if he no longer wanted me as his wife, but I couldn't live without him.

"Woman, do you never stop?" Stegthal broke into my thoughts. "Shaarvan, Shaarvan. It is all you say and all you think about every moment of the Tide. I have had enough of it," he shouted in an extremely nonShapechanger manner.

I looked up and met the fury in his eyes. I cowered, forgetting my bravery. Stegthal's fists were writhing — raging to be free. They were Isandor's hands, eager to paint my flesh with bruises.

"Stars. Never mind, Shaara. We shall continue to work on your projection. On board a ship, your sending out everything you think and feel will become most uncomfortable for the others. Already, it irritates *my* nerves."

Stegthal turned and stomped back into his office.

"I am sorry," I called after him.

He stopped, let out a groan, and said. "Shapechanger respect a woman's faithfulness. In that, at least, you are blameless." He said nothing more and returned to his packing.

My bondmates returned for more boxes. Stegthal lugged out another book-filled box, heaved it onto the table, glanced at me, and went back to his office.

Apparently, for the others, it was breaktime. My bondmates were getting drinks. Tenor asked me if I wanted one, and I nodded. Shaarac got a bottle, which he began to drink, although I could tell he wasn't hungry. He was far more interested in watching the guys, but if someone had tried to take away his milk, I was pretty sure Shaarac would wail.

The males were sweaty, having loaded and unloaded for hours. I think the sweat brought out their feelings even more than usual. Tenor, bringing over my drink, smelled tangy — the odor of worry. I picked up a bit of sour orange from Thedar, which was guilt. From Spelon, there was only his usual battle readiness — mustard. I absorbed such odors most of the time without thought. Processing them was a normal part of being a Shapechanger, but I was alert to such things even more so that day.

Spelon came over and sat down beside me. He held out his arms for Shaarac, and I handed him the baby. I wished I could stand and stretch, but Stegthal was in such a strange mood. His anger boiled his rage at me, a rotting pampa fruit accompanied by a yellow haze above him.

"Are you okay?" Spelon asked, patting my arm as if I were Shaarac's age.

I looked down so Spelon couldn't read me fully. I wondered what scent I was broadcasting. How did disillusion smell? Or panic? "No. I will never be well until my husband returns," I said.

Spelon frowned and shook his head. "Do not be stupid, woman. Your husband is here."

I glared tiredly. My energy was too low to blast him with something sharply hurtful like Tessa would have done. I would have moved away, but I was frozen to the seat by Stegthal's command. I merely sighed, let out an exasperated sound, and then added a second sigh for good measure.

But Spelon was playing with Shaarac. He probably hadn't even noticed my displeasure.

Enough. I was sick of the whole thing. I couldn't hold my tongue anymore. "You Shapechanger play silly games. I don't understand them. I obeyed Shaarvan's command in marrying Stegthal, but Shaarvan is the only husband I will ever have."

Spelon grabbed my wrist. "You dare much, woman. Stegthal . . ."

"Remove your hand from my wife." The words were stalactite daggers hurled across the room.

Spelon jerked away. Shaarac was startled by it and began to fuss, so Spelon rocked the baby up and down until my son was laughing again. When Spelon sat down once more, he took the farthest chair from where I was sitting.

Spelon had not meant to do anything wrong. He hadn't touched me in lust. I tried to defend him.

"Stegthal, Shaarvan never cared if . . ."

"Go to your room," Stegthal commanded. He had spoken to me using the possessive adjective appropriate for a slave, not the one that should have been used with a Shapechanger wife. The blood rushed from my brain and flooded my body. My head jerked erect. My eyes gave challenge. I could feel Change coming on.

"Shaara, stop," Thedar demanded. "There is no time for this. Obey Stegthal. We want you safe, and we shall allow nothing to interfere with that."

Thedar's eyes were not looking at me. They were focused on Stegthal. I could see that Thedar was as upset by the deliberate insult as I'd been. I breathed in deeply and headed for Spelon to take back my son. Stegthal flashed a Second Warning. I glanced at him, then turned and withdrew to my room.

A while later, Thedar came to speak to me. He entered the room and sat down on the bed beside me.

"As your bondmate, it is my right to command you," Thedar said. His voice was scratchy like he was unused to talking or was nervous.

I knew he had the right to command me. Shaarvan had told me so many times. Why did Thedar think I questioned it? I fidgeted, stretching my legs, then pulling them back again.

"I command you to listen, Shaara."

I nodded.

"It is time for us to go, Shaara. I shall be the one who takes you to the ship. But first, you and I will talk."

I opened my mouth to tell him I was not leaving Westla. A flash of Thedar's silent command stopped my words.

"I think Shaarvan was too easy on you."

Again, my mouth flew open, then shut.

"It was Shaarvan's right to deal with you as he saw fit. I am not criticizing it, but the freedoms he allowed are causing friction in your adaptation."

Thedar obviously knew nothing about my training with Shaarvan. He wasn't there all the times that Shaarvan had . . .

"Quiet your mind, woman. Your thoughts squirm like a nest of venomous serpents."

How could Thedar expect me to keep my thoughts obedient?

"You are rebellious. We all know that. If you were not so pleasing to look at, you would not get away with it."

I made the gesture for permission to speak.

Thedar shook his head. "Spelon and Tenor have asked me to talk to you. None of us want to see you hurt, but you need to know that we shall not interfere if you provoke Stegthal into beating you."

This was so unfair! I had done nothing to deserve his words.

"I have no interest in your self-pity, girl. Listen without it."

I gnawed at my lip in vexation.

"Emotion rules your existence, Shaara. That is normal for a female, I have been told, but you must begin using your brain. You have defied Stegthal at every turn, and he has been patient so far. But now, his anger does not seem propelled by your resistance. We believe he is becoming jealous of Shaarvan."

That brought my head up. Stegthal had no right . . .

"No, Shaara. He *has* the right. He is your husband. And he does not need to hear Shaarvan's name on every breath."

I let out a tea kettle of frustration.

"You must focus on the Primary, Shaara. Forget that you were once Shaarvan's. Concentrate on the present."

I shook my head. I wouldn't listen to this. How could Thedar expect me to?

"Shaarvan chose Stegthal to be your Second, Shaara. He must have had his reasons. Perhaps if you think on it, you can determine why he chose Stegthal for you."

Thedar raised my chin and stared into my eyes, probing. Whatever Thedar read in me, it seemed sufficient. He withdrew and continued. "It would be wise, Shaara, to accept what the stars have brought you.

"I doubt that any of us will have the opportunity to talk with you about Stegthal again, and you must be warned — he will not play games with you. If you push him any harder, he will beat you. You know that, and you think you can ignore it. But you are wrong, Shaara. It will not be like it was with Isandor.

If you push a Shapechanger into a rage, he will hurt you. Stegthal would not need to touch your body with his hand. He would hurt you in other ways. Did you not learn that with Shaarvan?"

My eyes were immediately awash with tears.

"Good. I have your attention. Remember the Primary. Shaarvan taught you its importance. So, you know the dangers of disobedience, and you know the rewards of compliance, but for some reason, you have not shifted your understanding of it to Stegthal. Have you not realized, Shaara, that the Primary means that it is *Stegthal* you must now, please?"

Once more, my eyes lifted to Thedar's.

"I have no interest, Shaara, in hearing you rant about unfairness. Stegthal is your husband. Accept that fact. *Please Stegthal*, or you will bear the consequences. Tenor, Spelon, and I do not wish to see you hurt, Shaara, but I repeat — we shall not interfere."

Thedar brushed back my hair and kissed my forehead. "Stegthal owns you, Shaara. Do not fight it. Adapt to it. You must."

Had Thedar allowed me to argue, my anger would have taken over, but the frustration of silence and the barrage of words pounding at me were more than I could tolerate. My tears flooded.

"Good. Tears are the beginnings and endings of a woman's distress. They are beneficial, Shaara. They will heal you."

For a moment, Thedar sat quietly. When I quieted, he ordered me to wash my face and use the facility. Then, he led me from my room.

The chambers were empty, the walls stripped of possessions, and all the boxes had disappeared. Stegthal and the others had left.

"Where is Shaarac?" I cried out.

"He is with the others onboard the ship. I will take you to him shortly, but I want you to understand that your life is in danger. There must be no arguments, Shaara. No temper tantrums, no discord of any kind. We must walk to the ship without drawing a speck of attention. For the first time, you will be unguarded, Shaara. No one must guess your position or your identity. And no one must know we are fleeing Westla."

I bowed my head. They had won. If Shaarac was onboard the ship, I couldn't refuse to go.

"You must change in to Westlan clothing," Thedar said, handing me a dress. "We shall pretend that you are my wife. We will walk through the corridors as quietly and unobtrusively as possible."

I took the dress from him and started to return to my room, but he shook his head, turned me around, and lifted the lavender over my head. Nakedness embarrassed me, but Thedar was all business. He slipped the Westlan dress on me, buttoned up the back, and then checked me over, glancing down at my shoes, and smoothing my hair.

"Good. I am armed, Shaara, with several weapons. If we are attacked, I will put you in the chest hold, and you must remain still and silent. Do not move — no matter what happens."

I nodded in compliance.

"Pretend well, *Stella*," he ordered.

I smiled at the name change. Thedar did not return it. His eyes burned with seriousness.

As we left Stegthal's dwelling and moved into the halls, Thedar's arm circled me, playing the husband. His lips dropped to my neck, and he kissed me. I stifled my protest.

"Easy, Stella," he whispered in my ear as we continued. "Loosen up your body. You are stiff with indignation. This is only a pretense. I am your bondmate. I shall do nothing to hurt you."

I relaxed a little then, but I was nervous. I didn't understand why the others had left me alone with Thedar, even if I did trust him.

I could feel a pipe weapon poking me at times. Westla outlawed weapons. How could Thedar have one?

We walked by several groups of young males. They stared at Thedar with open envy and examined me with lustful eyes. I shivered, tinged with fear.

"They will not bother us," Thedar assured me each time, and he brushed his lips across my forehead or smoothed back my hair with a gentle caress.

One group followed us for a bit. I heard them discussing things that made me blush. Thedar looked down at me suddenly and then stopped and turned to face them.

"She is young and innocent, lords. You upset her. Do you not have sufficient money to appease your needs?"

They issued quick apologies, drank me in with their eyes, and then slipped away.

Otherwise, our trip was uneventful. We passed three or four couples, several more groups of young males, and a few single Shapechanger. They all passed by us courteously or hastened off in opposite directions. No one seemed to be watching us or harboring murderous thoughts.

Thedar's clasp was not as tight as Shaarvan's or Stegthal's, yet it was firm. Although he set a steady pace, it was comfortable. The long halls were soon behind us, and I could smell the antiseptic space quarantine area up ahead. Leaving Westla was easier than entering — no inspections or spray downs, only long paths to follow.

As we passed through the final group of silver tunnels, my stomach began to rumble. Having been robbed of breakfast and lunch, it complained with several noisy growls. Thedar chuckled, patted my stomach and hurried me forward.

He knew exactly where the ship was docked. Once there, I would have paused a moment to admire the beauty of the ship, but Thedar firmly urged me forward. We ascended the ramp and stepped inside. The door closed behind us. At once, the motors flared up, and in seconds, we were lifting up and out of the Saberey eye of the space tunnel.

I was very happy to see my son safe in Tenor's arms. I held my hands out and silently begged Stegthal. His eyes narrowed as he looked at me. "Did she give you any trouble, Thedar?"

"No," he said. "I explained what was necessary and why. Shaara did exactly as she was ordered."

"I see." Stegthal handed me my son and turned to stare out at the stars.

I hugged and kissed my son. I had not liked the separation. Shaarac put up with my show of affection, but he was more interested in taking in his surroundings. He looked big-eyed with wonder. My eyes followed his.

This ship was different than any I'd ever seen. I'd noticed that from the outside when Thedar led me towards it. He'd told me the ship belonged to Stegthal. I was curious about how different it was from the one that Shaarvan had flown to Westla.

Westlan and Altarian ships were mostly pyramid or mushroom-shaped with tiger-eye insignias. I'd seen copper-hued ships, the dull black of carrier ships, and the shiny silver of the fastest luxury flitters, but Stegthal's ship was nothing like any of them. It was egg-shaped, slightly green on the outside, and had markings that bore no Shapechanger design I'd ever seen.

Why did Stegthal own a ship anyway, and what did he use it for? I gazed at the control room interface. No one was monitoring the panel. Where was the crew? Who was piloting the ship? I had a thousand questions on the tip of my tongue, but I had no time to ask them.

"Take the boy, Spelon. He is yawning. He can be put to bed now."

Spelon's eyes swept over me. His eyes were neutral. I could read nothing from them. He walked over to me and took Shaarac into his arms. My son yawned again. As Spelon left, my eyes followed them.

"Come here, Girl," Stegthal ordered.

I obeyed, but even that didn't seem to satisfy Stegthal. His hand seized my neck. "It is good that Thedar's report was favorable. It would take little to enrage me."

I froze. Did I dare speak? Would it help or hurt?

"No, I prefer your silence. It is far less argumentative."

I dropped my eyes, but I couldn't still my thoughts.

Stegthal laughed. "You scolded her, didn't you, Thedar? See how much good it did? Her mind still gives battle. Perhaps Shaarvan should have given her to Spelon. He has a Warrior's disposition."

"Shaarvan had his reasons, Stegthal."

Stegthal moved one of his fingers. The movement shifted my head until I was staring up into his eyes. He studied my face as if seeing it for the first time.

"I am not a combatant, girl. There will be no war between us. You will obey me, or you will spend long periods of time in our room alone and without entertainment."

His hold on me did not allow me to nod. Perhaps he read acquiescence in my thoughts. Suddenly, he swept me up into his arms.

"Thedar, the ship is underway now. It needs no guidance or maintenance. Your quarters are on the second level. Make yourself at home. I shall be busy for the next few hours."

So saying, Stegthal carried me to our new dwelling.

Chapter Six

Thedar, onboard Stegthal's ship

Earlier, I had been given no time to explain to the others that I disagreed with Stegthal. Perhaps Spelon and Tenor would not have liked my arguing with him, but Stegthal's tone with Shaara was more than I could permit.

We had all felt Stegthal's anger with the girl. No doubt she had challenged him beyond his tolerance. It happened at times with newly captive girls, but a male knew that when his patience was exhausted, he must leave her side and permit the rage to recede.

Stegthal had not done so. Instead, he had lashed out at her, not with violence, but with an assault even more crushing to her nature. She had reacted to the slight, as one would expect. No Shapechanger woman deserved that kind of affront. Shaara was not a slave. She was a Trendacons with generations of the highest and most powerful DNA. She was the wife of two Warlords and a mother. There was no rationalization for such abuse.

Yet, when I began to withdraw from the scene to compose myself and prepare what I would say to him, Stegthal halted me and asked for my assistance. His request surprised me.

Of course, I was willing to escort his wife to the ship. I could see that Stegthal had thought out his plan. He said it would be dangerous for Shaara to be seen in his company. Thenos' spies would probably have already marked him as Shaara's Second. That, I understood and appreciated, but why had he chosen me as the girl's guardian for the trip?

Why not the rightful next in line, which was Spelon? He was the better warrior if such were needed. I found it puzzling, and it concerned me that jealousy might have distorted Stegthal's sense of order and custodianship.

However, I said nothing and agreed. Then, I withdrew and continued lugging the heavy boxes to the robot platform outside the dwelling. I passed Spelon and Tenor several times, but they were as busy as I was.

As I continued the toil, I thought over the conversation. It was good that Stegthal chose me to escort his wife. It gave me the opportunity that I had long desired — to talk privately with Shaara. She was a smart girl. I was sure that a few words about the Primary would steer her on a better course. I thought it might also curb her natural impulses to whine about Shaarvan's absence. Yet, I did not want to be present when Stegthal told Spelon of the decision.

When the boxes were almost all loaded, I went to Stegthal's bed chamber. As always, Shaara was mercurial. Yet, I think behind those lovely rebellious eyes of hers, her brain began to register the sense of my arguments. As I thought, her loyalty to Shaarvan had not allowed her to recognize that the Primary applied to Stegthal. Shaara can be obstinate, but in general, she has a sweet nature, and she adapts well. I hope she will do better in the future.

And our trip had gone well. No rebellion on her part. She was excellently behaved. We all agree that Shaara is very special. We recognize her potential and want her wellbeing. My time alone with her will be carried with me always. Although I would never have taken advantage of the situation, I found pleasure in being with her.

I suppose it is strange to have agreed to be a bondmate with a female I can never own, but I am grateful for the opportunity. She is worth it, even if she will always be no more than a daughter/sister. But I, like the others, already adore her. My love for her, although not the same kind of love that Shaarvan must feel, has a strength that is solid and constant.

But now, relieved of my burden (which could truthfully never be considered a burden but a moment of closeness with Shaara,) I must set out to make my peace with Spelon. I must let him know that I recognize his position and that it was not my choice to oppose his rights.

Of course, that will not reduce his constant opposition to Stegthal, but it may help to relieve his anxiety concerning me. There must never be strife between the three of us. As if we were military, rank is everything. I am sure he knows that, but reassurance is a good thing.

Stegthal is another matter. We must watch him. Something is amiss there. Perhaps Spelon is right.

Shaara, onboard Thal's ship

Stegthal did not beat me. He rode me fiercely, but there was no doubt my body accepted him. Webbed in like a rodeo calf, my mind fought, but his touch enthralled. Afterward, he seemed pleased, and when I cried, he rose up, chuckling, and left without a word.

Later, when we ate lunch together, when he served me, he was gentle and even teased me with a smile. And, although when he sat beside me, his arm possessively slid around my waist, he did not fondle me in front of the others or insult me as he had done earlier.

I thought that meant I'd avoided all retaliation, but the very next Tide, Stegthal declared he was name-changing us. Stegthal was to be called Thal in the future, I was to be referred to as Thalia, and Shaarac was henceforth christened Thaarac.

"My name is Shaara," I babbled out like an idiot, not understanding why Stegthal would choose to change our names.

All eyes centered on me. The disapproval in them was evidently unanimous.

"It is the husband who chooses a wife's name," Tenor informed me.

"Tessa said that Shaara was a name of power," I countered.

Thal picked up my hand. I shivered at his touch (and not with the thrill of it). His eyes met mine. "Thalia means power in Stenorian," he told me. "Stenori is my planet, and so, now, it is yours."

"Thalia. I like it," Thedar said. "It fits her." Thedar's eyes on me urged me to remember the Primary.

How many times would I be renamed? Was it important? At least it was better than being called *girl* or *child*. "Is that where we are going? Stenori?" I asked.

A sudden silence, the shaking of heads. All eyes grew stern or troubled. Had I erred again?

"No, it is not where we are going. But you are a woman, Thalia. Must I remind you of that again? You have no need to know our destination."

I winced at Thal's rudeness, but I kept my eyes down. After a moment, I asked if I could go get Thaarac."

"No," Thal barked, speaking with such force the chamber echoed with it. His hand seized my neck. "Spelon is with Thaarac. Our son is fine."

Ignoring me, Thal continued his conversation with the others. He discussed the motors of the ship and their maintenance. I sat there, brewing with hatred and anger. Thedar's eyes found mine. He shook his head.

Thedar was right, but it was so difficult. He didn't have to endure Thal's insults or the bed assaults.

The words of the males switched to another language. I couldn't understand them. I wondered why Thal required my presence. If I were a slave, I could have been put to work, but they didn't allow that. They wouldn't even permit me to take care of my own son. Instead, they made me sit around like an ornament. What value did I have to any of them?

Thal broke off in the middle of his sentence to stare down at me. "You are of value, Thalia. You are our greatest treasure. You — and the others of your station and gender — hold our future. You bear and nurture our sons. It is not because we find you unworthy that we shield you. It is our Shapechanger code. To cherish and provide for you is our responsibility for the future of the Shapechanger."

I was embarrassed. I hadn't spoken, yet I'd disturbed them. Again, I dropped my eyes, but Thal's eyes did not leave me. He released my neck and raised my chin.

After a moment, Thal nodded. "Thedar, you are right."

What had Thedar said to Thal?

Thal smiled down at me. "We were discussing Deadstar, Thalia. It will be our new home."

"Deadstar?" I should have been more cautious, but I couldn't help the questions that came gushing out. "Where is it? What's it like? When will we get there?"

A crinkle appeared in the sides of Thal's eyes, and then he laughed. "Shaarvan warned me you would question me to death."

I bit my lip. I should have known better than to do that with a Shapechanger.

"Look up, Thalia," Thal said. "I am not angry. Questions are the sign of a keen mind. I had forgotten your intelligence. For a while, I saw you only as a woman.

"Thedar, I admit I have erred. I do not know why I did not see it. Of course, Thalia obeys when you explain things to her. She has the questioning mind of a scientist. I have been a prejudiced fool."

The others did not like his admitting that in front of me. I was aware of their reactions, but I was more interested in reading Thal. The depths of him were hard for me to reach, but I figured he should be easier, having more deeply bonded me. I probed.

Thal threw back his head and laughed. The sound went through the ship's hollow chamber like a sonic bomb. The others and I all jumped.

"Thalia, you dare much when you enter into a male's thoughts. Your mind is as delicate as the hand I hold. It could be crushed so easily. Not one of us would harm you — *intentionally*. But . . . Do not probe us, Child. It is dangerous."

My eyes lowered. Thal hadn't needed to scold me. The headache I'd received from my attempt was warning enough.

"Tenor, take her to Thaarac before she decides to take us on in physical combat!" Thal joked.

They all laughed. I rose up, red in the face, my head hurting, my pride wounded — but I walked to the door with my chin up and my shoulders back.

"Thalia," Thal called out to me.

I stopped and turned around.

"There is respect in our eyes as we laugh," Thal said.

I didn't know what to say. I stood a moment, staring at him. He winked at me before he turned back to the others.

How many layers did Stegthal, I mean Thal, have? He showed me one, and the next was totally different. As I walked away, I heard the sound of his laughter thundering out again.

Spelon, onboard Thal's ship

It is an agony to share the ship with her. She babbles of nothing and then flashes those tiny pearl-like teeth. I cannot focus clearly when she does that. Her lips part, and my mind carries me to the room down below, where I would drag her in a moment if her status were different. Then, when I pull my thoughts away from such unseemly but pleasurable fantasies, she is biting at her lip in worry, and my eyes are once more drowning in hers.

She tosses questions at us as if she were a young boy skipping pebbles across the water's surface. I think, sometimes, that she does not listen to the answers we give her, but then she speaks, and I see that she has assimilated it, but in a manner that only half makes sense. She twists everything about with such illogic that one can scarcely trace its path.

I can ignore the feminine tosses of her hair. I do not need to look at the way the colors intertwine. I am a Warrior. I can look away. I do not need to observe how the ship's light causes strands of her curls to light up like gold. The softness of her voice does not need to tease my senses. I do not have to compare the rhythms of her words to the notes of a concert. Yet I do, and it irritates me.

In truth, everything she does aggravates me — the way she cocks her head when she hears something she does not accept, the widening of her eyes when she is surprised, and the closing of them. Her eyelashes are ridiculously long and flirtatious.

I hate the manner of her walk — those dainty little steps in feet no bigger than one's hand. All of her annoys me, but not as much as Thal's possession of her — his arm across her shoulder, the way he fondles her neck in warning or for his own pleasure, or his touch on her face, his lips on hers . . .

Why did Shaarvan give her to Thal? Why did he honor a scholar over a Warrior? Why did Shaarvan not choose to give her to me?

I should have refused my friend. I should have told him I had better things to do than guard his wife. Why did I agree to this madness? How can I endure being trapped on this ship with her when the smell of her fills a room with desire?

I have taken over the training of my mates. I shall prevent them from becoming lazy in their prowess. It is a thing I am good at, and also it will keep my mind off Thal's wife. I shall spend my Tides practicing throws and armored battle readiness.

None of my mates can compete with me. They are not Elite Warriors, but I shall make them so. Even Thal, I shall push him beyond his limit. They will all be worthy guards of Thalia when I am through.

I would like to bar her from the exercise room. She does not belong there with the sweat and heaving of males. Yet, Thal has granted her free rein to roam the ship. She does not come near me when I am alone. She knows my fierceness will bring her to tears. It is necessary.

Do the others know how I feel about her? Do I give myself away?

Thalia, onboard Thal's ship

One morning, I discovered Thal pouring over his research. His computer was installed, and there were cables going everywhere.

"What are you doing?" I asked. "What are the cables for? You didn't have them on Westla."

"Ah, the inquisitive one is back," he kidded me.

I could tell he was pleased I'd visited. I'd already explored every place but his computer area. I'd actually only come to ask him where my books were stored, but what Thal was doing looked far more interesting.

"Come look at this, Thalia," he said.

I moved closer and peered into the computer. He had set it up like a telescope, just like he'd done on Westla.

"Is that the space directly outside the ship?"

"Yes, remember the nova I showed you before? This one is far more recent. It is close. It went nova only a thousand Passes ago!"

I sighed, then stared some more. It was pretty. "That's what I don't understand about astronomy," I said after a moment, plopping myself down on a chair beside Thal. "Astronomy is supposed to be a modern science, but it deals only with history! I want to know what is happening now, not before I was born and back in ancient times!"

Thal laughed, then nodded his head as if thinking about it. "So would all astronomers, Thalia, but how can we do that?"

He was asking *me* a question. I bit my lip, then smiled at him. "Maybe . . . you could make a telescope that time-traveled so it shows you what was actually happening when the star went Nova . . . But that would still be in the past." I paused and reconsidered. "I guess you could locate stars that were showing signs of going Nova and journey closer."

"That we do, but they are all distant and their light . . ."

"Then why don't we just go there?"

Thal laughed and reached out to push back a lock of my hair. "Because I am babysitting my wife."

I turned away. I hadn't meant to irritate him. I waited for permission to leave.

"Thalia," he said, grabbing my hand and pulling me back towards him. "I did not mean to wound you. It has been a long time since I have been with a woman. I forget how easily your gender is hurt with words."

It was nice of him to apologize if that's what he'd been doing. But his apology brought up another question I'd been meaning to ask. "Why do you always say things like that? You talk like you're old."

"I am old," he said, chuckling.

I didn't respond. I studied a mound of books leaning against the wall and an empty space that looked like it was just waiting for him to heap research papers on it. On the side of the room were his collection of antique charts. I'd seen them before, but I knew I wasn't allowed to touch them.

It was all interesting, but if Thal wanted to play games with my mind, I would leave. I stood up to march out, prepared to stomp my feet a bit as I departed, just to let him know how offended I was.

He watched me for a moment, probably reading my thoughts. "Thalia, do you know who Besnordaf was?"

I sighed. "Yes. He was an astronomer Shaarvan mentioned. A lot. Shaarvan said that Besnordaf traveled to exotic worlds where the people did not look like us."

"Besnordaf is *my* true name."

I spun around to stare at him. "You are named after the astronomer?"

"I *am* Besnordaf."

I shook my head, convinced again that Thal was teasing me. "That's absurd! Shaarvan said Besnordaf discovered a galaxy sixty Passes ago."

"Sixty-six Passes ago, I found Worthnep. I was thirty-two then."

I closed my mouth. It had fallen open in disbelief. Shapechanger did not lie. But . . . "Thal, I don't understand how you can lie and not get sick, but your fabrication is not even the least bit funny."

Thal stood, reached out, and took my hand. He led me back to his chair and pulled me down into his lap.

"When I was ninety-three, Thalia, I shot off into space, heading for unexplored territories. I had decided that I had lived long enough and that I might as well die going somewhere new. I headed for a black hole, thinking it would be an interesting way to leave this Plane of Existence."

That couldn't be true. Thal didn't look old, and now he was saying that he'd been ninety-three? Nothing made sense. I examined his face, looking for age spots or wrinkles or . . .

"The hole I headed for was a small one, and close to it was an alien race called the Kloog. I never made it to the black hole. The Kloog were far too interesting to leave. They repaired my aging cells and made me young again. I stayed with them two Passes before they sent me home. Being young again is like living twice."

Thal's story seemed ridiculous. I shook my head in disbelief. "You're making this up, right?"

He smiled, then shook his head. "A Shapechanger cannot lie, remember?"

It was absolutely preposterous, but it did answer some of the questions I'd had about Thal. In fact, it explained a lot, including why Tessa had called him an old man. How had she known?

"Is that really, really true?" I asked, searching his eyes for even a hint of a smile.

"Truth."

"Did Shaarvan know?"

Thal nodded. "Yes, but your bondmates do not."

"Shaarvan married me to an ancient?"

Thal laughed. "Only my brain, inquisitive one. My body is no more than Shaarvan's age — as you have discovered."

Thal's look made me blush. I looked down and studied my fingernails as if they could center my thoughts. "I must bore you," I said. "No wonder you call me a child."

Thal laughed. "You do not bore me at all. You bring me rapture."

His hands had begun to explore my body. I wiggled out of his lap and stood up.

"I think Thaarac must be waking now. I shall go to him — if that is OK?"

Thal laughed, not the booming laugh of thunder that he sometimes issued, but a new low chuckle he was developing, one that sent chills up and down my spine.

"Run, Thalia, scurry from your fear of me."

I turned, but I wasn't quick enough. Once more, he caught me and pulled me back.

"I was teasing you, my dear. You are safe, no need to run. It is the nights that Shapechanger prefer for prowling and for joining."

My face heated. My throat went dry.

As I left, I heard his laughter follow me.

I checked on Thaarac, although I figured he'd still be napping. He was. His mouth was curved into an adorable little smile, and, for once, his finger wasn't red from his insistent sucking. It lay close by, ready as needed. I smoothed the blanket around Thaarac and tiptoed away.

Thal was right. He did frighten me. I had never found any enjoyment with Isandor's possession of me. I had endured it because I had no other choice, but Thal pleasured me. The fact embarrassed me. I loved Shaarvan with all my soul, yet lately, I found myself lusting for Thal. And I hated myself for it. I was weak and unworthy of Shaarvan. I didn't know what to do about it either because it wasn't like I could tell Stegthal to stop. I brushed a tear from my eye and started walking.

I felt restless and — lonely. The ship seemed empty. I had prowled through all the chambers open to me, only barred from a few. My bondmates seemed distant now. I felt shut out. Thal I feared, and the others rejected me. It hurt to be the solitary female, the only one without a friend.

I went to complain to Tenor about it. He was sitting in the common room, studying a file of papers. He made no move to hide them from me, but a glance at them told me they were the usual legal stuff he was always pondering. Tenor didn't dabble only with Westlan rulings but investigated the laws of other planets. Apparently, although most planets used Shapechanger law as their backbone, their interpretations varied. Tenor explained a little of it to me, but he said that a woman did not need to delve into such matters. I hadn't bothered to argue. What was the point?

Tenor enjoyed talking about some things and wasn't adverse to giving me long-winded lectures on certain legalities. Sometimes, bits and pieces were interesting, but at the moment, I wasn't feeling like getting a personalized dose of law school.

"Why do you guys avoid me now?" I asked as I plopped down beside him. "Have I been so bad that my presence is offensive?"

Tenor didn't answer, but he flipped his folder closed and shifted to look at me.

He was smiling, so I continued. "I enter a room, and if you guys are all talking, you stop. If you are playing a game, you put it away, and when you laugh and wrestle, you break off if I enter the room. It's as if I have a contagious disease you don't want to come in contact with!"

Tenor laughed and shook his head. "We enjoy your company, Thalia. We do not avoid you. But your husband is not pleased when we gather around you. We will not quarrel with him over you."

Tenor turned his face away from me so I couldn't read his eyes. I knew he wanted me to leave, yet I persisted. "Shaarvan said I could *always* talk with you. He said you would be . . ."

Abruptly, Tenor turned back to face me. His eyes darkened. "Thal is your husband now, and he does not like our friendship."

I stood up, stamped my foot, and turned to leave. How short were the memories of males! "I am not Thal's! I belong to Shaarvan. I will always belong to Shaarvan."

"Does she never stop that?" Spelon asked, thumping his way into both the room and our conversation. He clapped Tenor on the back, and I suddenly felt a stab of jealousy for their closeness. We used to be friends (almost) like that.

As if to rub acid on my wounds, Spelon added, "Thalia, your tongue needs new words. Try *Thal*." He rammed himself down on the bench and then started poking Tenor in the ribs, reminding him it was time for a training session.

I shot Spelon an evil glare and opened my mouth to say something nasty. If only I could think of something that wouldn't get me in trouble.

Tenor gave me a look of warning. It was frustrating that he knew me so well. I closed my mouth and just glared at Spelon. I figured that was safer.

"Thal has renamed you," Tenor said. "He has claimed you in a deep bond. He has full rights as your husband. The Primary is his."

I stared at Tenor and then at Spelon, who was nodding his head vigorously. Then I raised my chin and vowed to them, "I will always belong to Shaarvan, *only* Shaarvan."

Spelon threw back his head and laughed. "Once Thal finally gets around to beating your little bottom, Woman, you will *finally* know who your owner is. And I look forward to it because then we will not have to hear you proclaiming the same litany every Tide!"

Something caught fire in me. It wasn't Spelon's words, exactly. It was more than that. It was like none of them believed Shaarvan would ever come back. Spelon was just the final push that broke my patience.

The anger in me flared. I stamped my foot, and I Changed. I didn't know I was going to until I roared.

Thal rushed in almost instantly and ordered the others out.

"Thalia," he said, "I did not know you were at Level Five. This is delightful. We shall complete our Second bonding."

I didn't understand. My tail beat on the ground angrily. I wished Thal had not chased Spelon away. I had looked forward to scratching a claw mark or two on his cheeks.

I was still thinking of how delicious it would feel to pay Spelon back for his rudeness when I heard the snarl behind me. Thal had Changed, too. His Saberey cat was huge — and displayed beautiful coloring. I admired the markings on his face. My tongue was eager to lick at his whiskers, but coloring was not enough. He might be unworthy of me. I roared. My claws raked the air.

The male hunkered down and batted at me playfully. I swiped at his chest, but he was too fast. He sprang at me, knocking me down, then rolled me onto my side.

His purr was loud in my ear. "You are charming, my dear," his thoughts tumbled at me. I growled deep and low, spurning his human voice. Again, my paw swept out. My claws almost scratched his shoulder, but he swung away. Once more, he pounced. He weighed twice what I did. I fell in a heap with him on top of me.

His great mouth seized my neck. I growled again and struggled to stand. His teeth sank deeper. I froze. I hadn't given up, though. If he loosened even a moment, I'd be up and away. For a moment, his teeth shook my skin, and then they sank in more powerfully. I wanted to nip him back, to rip his throat until the blood pooled on the floor, but he was grinding his teeth in my throat. If I didn't submit, it would be my blood flowing onto the floor.

The pain of the male's teeth and the knowledge of the strength of his jaw forced a whimper out of me. It was what he'd been waiting for. He freed me and licked my face, a statement of forgiveness for my challenge. He could afford to be generous. I'd submitted and accepted him as my mate.

He bit me sharply, then on the side, demanding that I stand. I knew what was coming. I growled low, but it was not in warning. As he took me, I didn't fight him. I'd already accepted him as my mate.

I refused to listen at first when Thal tried to bridge me back to my other form. I was a tiger. What use had I for other shapes? He seized my neck and bit, reminding me of his dominance. Only then did I obey.

Yet once I began transitioning back, I was terrified. What if I did it wrong and ended up half and half? My panic lasted only a moment. My Change went smoothly, as automatic as breathing. And after, Thal held me in his arms and reassured me, telling me how well I'd done.

"But I almost didn't come back," I said. "I wanted to stay a beast forever!"

"Thalia, there is no need to be afraid. I shall always guide you and keep you safe."

I wasn't crying, but the lump of need was there. I took a breath and held it for a moment. It calmed me.

"How did you know I'd Changed, Thal? How did you know to come?"

"I felt it. I shall always feel your need. Although I hope you will not allow your anger to push you into Change."

He had not asked me why I'd turned into a cat. Did he know? Would he punish me?

Thal tightened his hold on me slightly. His lips left delightful kisses on my neck. I groaned.

He chuckled, more a purr than a laugh. "No," he said, "I shall not punish you, Thalia. Not this time. But I want you to Change again, now before your fear makes it a hurdle. You must practice switching back and forth so that in the future there is no danger of your getting stuck in your alter image."

I did not want to Change, but I obeyed. Over and over, we Changed until the process was no more difficult than the blink of an eye.

When Thal was satisfied, we rested. I lay my head against his chest and listened to his heartbeat.

"What were you wearing, Thalia, before you first Changed?" Thal asked casually.

It was only then I realized my clothes were gone. Why hadn't I noticed before? I covered myself with my hands, but it didn't do much good. "Where's my dress? And my shoes?"

Thal laughed and pushed my hands away. "Do not hide from me, Thalia. I have held your body for many Tides and seen you unclothed for an equal number. You are my wife."

My tiger memories of not needing clothing helped somewhat to relieve my inhibitions, but I continued glancing about the room, searching for the missing clothes.

"You will not find them, Thalia. They disappear in the Change."

Thal didn't seem concerned. He stood, picked up his shirt, and draped it over me. "I suggest, my dear, since nakedness bothers you, that until you learn how to keep your clothes on, you should probably not Change in front of the others."

Thal's shirt was huge, hanging down to my calves. The sleeves dangled, hiding my hands. Not a good look on me, I guessed, but I was grateful for the cover.

"But how can I Change and keep my clothes on? How did you?" I asked.

Thal gripped the shirt with his fist. "Try holding on to your dress, like this, when you Change. That worked for me at first. In time, you will learn to transition without clinging to your clothes, and then you can include your shoes in the focus as well."

I nodded, then reached up and pressed a kiss on Thal's cheek. It was the first time I'd ever done so.

He smiled, but his bare chest was distracting me. I looked away.

"Is it true we are landing on Deadstar tomorrow?"

Thal's eyes flared. "Who told you that?"

One of my hands had disobeyed me and was touching the pectorals of his chest. The hardness of his muscle structure was an enjoyable texture.

"No one. I read it when I Changed . . . and I didn't probe."

"Level Six and rising." Thal's eyes studied me with a curious look.

I dropped my hand and flushed.

"Thalia, if you were disappointed by our interaction in our altered shape, I shall be happy to satisfy you in this body."

"No," I whispered.

He nodded thoughtfully. "I shall not press you, Thalia, but I am not averse to your initiating desire. A woman's needs are always her husband's responsibility.

That was new to me and something to think about.

Thal turned me about, and we walked toward our chamber, luckily without meeting the others. I quickly water-showered. A clean dress was waiting for me when I walked out, as was Thal.

"Get dressed," he said. "The more Power you get, the safer it becomes for you, but Power requires training. Tessa sent some exercises to work on. It is time we start them."

Thenos, in the Palace on Altar

It has been a manyTide since I have heard news of my princess. Chaslow, the fool, blew up the nursery where Shaarvan's son was supposed to be staying, but the idiot missed the baby! Curses on the Somber Tree, how could he be so inept?

And, even worse, in doing so, he scared Shaara into hiding. Chaslow says he has searched Westla and cannot find her. But there are underground tunnels and caverns in the interior of the planet. My uncle may have hidden her in one. He has always favored Shaarvan over me. In time, I shall dispose of Tem also.

Shaara must still be on Westla. Where else would they have taken her?

The Old Ones could be hiding her. She is a Trendacons, but so am I. Would they take sides against me in this? But perhaps they do not know she is mine now. Should I converse with them? No, Shaarvan is their heir. They would not help me — unless he were dead. And I have not managed that yet.

Curse the stars! What am I to do? How will I find her?

Chaslow says he fears for his life. Why does he think I care for his worthless soul? He deserves to die. He has ruined everything! Even my dirtwalkers would not have failed me as badly as Chaslow has.

I have no peace without my princess. Everything has turned bitter. All of Altar disturbs me with its problems. It is contemptible that Shaarvan landed without my princess and failed to die. But even worse, now he flaunts my authority. He refuses to come to the Great Hall and hear his judgment. Even when the proclamation of his death was tolled, he dodged my peons and escaped into the Untouched Territories. No one is allowed to go there without a permit, yet he broke Altarian law to hide in the caverns like a common criminal. It is an embarrassment.

And my woes do not end there. Shaarvan had the audacity to set up some kind of base where he can plot against me. He has weapons and people with him, hundreds, I am told — Shapechanger and Commoners alike. My own mother, Tevor, Starnkor, and my brother Pathe, whom I saved from the peons when they would have destroyed him, all have aligned against me. How dare they! Four times, I have sent a retaliatory force to end their uprising, but each time, only my Commoners died.

How does this look to have my own family opposing me? And the remaining elite of Altar have allies from other planets. Everywhere, I feel eyes against me — spies, infiltrators, and assassins. It is maddening and, dare I say it, hurtful.

The Shapechanger forces cannot touch me, of course. I have doubled my guard. But the indignity of it! And those eyes shadowing me everywhere . . .

Why is everyone critical of me? Why do they turn on me? Can they not see what magnificent plans I have for the future of Altar? Do they not realize I shall bring back the glory of the Shapechanger?

It does not matter. I shall crush them, Shapechanger and Commoner alike. I shall execute them, one by one. First Shaarvan, then Pathe, Starnkor, Tevor, and last of all, my mother. I shall be sad to have her put to death. Shaara likes her. But no one may stand in my way. I am Thenos, Emperor, King of Altar, and soon to be the ruler of all the Leagues.

My princess will understand. She will see I had to do it to save Altar. She will see how good and kind I am. She will sit in my lap with her arms about me, and her lips will play on mine. Her long, luscious curls shall drape my . . .

I am hard. Stars! It has been a TwentyTide since I felt the urge to take a girl. The thought of Shaara has given me back my maleness. My blessed princess.

I shall search for you, Shaara. I know you want me. They have forced you to hide from me, but I shall find you. Do not worry. I have reached your mind several times. I shall continue to do so. No matter the cost, I shall bring you home, my sweet, sweet Shaara.

Thal, onboard the ship

My wife believes that I shall soon be bored with her. How wrong she is. She is the freshness of a new star, an unexplored world or an uncharted comet, and I revel in the mystery of her.

I admit I was surly with the child when we were forced to leave Westla. My attitude was unseemly, as Thedar let me know. He defended her well and rightly.

What was it that caused me to lose my patience with her? Perhaps it was the fear of losing her. The snow path she had found was impressive. Without Tessa, could I have saved her? I do not think so. Even with my Passes of collected knowledge, I have seen nothing equal to it.

And then, of course, there is her nonstop prattle of Shaarvan. He is her every waking thought — comparisons, memories, lessons she has learned, words he has taught her. It is as if she were not whole without him. That wears on me, but it is to be expected. Do we Shapechanger not honor constancy? Do we not praise loyalty?

I shall not tell her yet that she carries my son. She has only sketchy memories of that night. I think it best. I have ordered the others not to inform her, either. She does not need another shock. Our relationship is tenuous enough without what she will consider an added horror. I shudder to think of her searching for that path of snow again.

I shall have several Tides before she knows. Shapechanger women have no monthly flow. The ship will hide any discomfort she might feel. It will supply her nutritional needs and calm her with non-harmful herbs. (I shall make sure to bring a supply of them with us to Deadstar.)

I would not have seeded her with a child had not Tessa demanded it, but the idea now gives me indescribable delight. A child of Thalia cannot help but be rich with Power. He will be a great Warrior, as well. Spelon will see to that through his training rituals. The stars have shone favorably on my house, and I am grateful. To possess a woman like Thalia and, soon, a son . . .

Thalia, onboard Thal's ship

Deadstar from space is a beautiful, green planet. As we sat around the table finishing off our breakfast, I stared at it and questioned the others. I wanted to know why it had been named Deadstar, but no one knew. Tenor and Thedar shook their heads and shrugged their shoulders, indicating they didn't care. Spelon growled about my asking stupid questions, but Thal smiled, approval in his eyes. He promised me we would access the computer databanks.

"Do they have landoors there?" I wanted to know.

"Do you wish me to shut her up?" Spelon asked, rotating his chair as if he were about to lurch forward.

Thal shifted his gaze to Spelon and cleared his throat with an almost tigerish growl but otherwise ignored him. "I think they have stubras, Thalia, which are very like landoors."

I smiled at Thal, then asked what else he knew about Deadstar.

We landed on the north side of the planet, setting down just as if there'd been a spaceport there, but, of course, there wasn't since Deadstar had no inhabitants. The ramp lowered and with Spelon and Tenor in the lead, we stepped onto Deadstar. Thaarac's little eyes were as wide open with interest as mine as I carried him down the ramp. The others, loaded pipes ready and on alert, seemed indifferent to the fact that it was a new and exciting adventure we were commencing.

The air smelled delightful, especially after the containment of the ship. The planet's fragrance was the sweetness of many blooming plants. A gentle breeze caressed my cheek delightfully.

The vista from the ramp was equally pleasant. Grasses covered the space about us, and an expanse of heavy-branched trees grew to the left. On the right, a gentle hill with low bushy plants and large bright orange blooms was probably the cause of the delicious-smelling air.

We walked forward cautiously. Although the planet had been well-scanned by an automated scouting fleet a thirteenPass before, my bondmates were on high alert. The info banks stated that Deadstar lacked any large predators, but Thal told us that, sometimes, scouts were dangerously wrong, and a few exploratory settlements, who'd based their decisions on such information, had been decimated by hibernating carnivores awakened to the smell of warm flesh.

When Spelon and Tenor stepped off the ramp, they zigzagged forward, investigating. I thought the rest of us would be allowed to explore, too, but Thal made my son and me sit at the bottom of the ramp while he and Thedar stood towering over us, watchful and battle-ready.

Thaarac cried because none of his friends wanted to play. I jiggled him up and down and spoke quietly to him, but he wouldn't stop fretting. He was fighting me for his freedom, wanting to crawl about. Thal spoke sharply and threatened to make me go inside. I tried even harder then, but Thaarac had a mind of his own. His anger grew louder.

Thedar offered to take Thaarac, but Thal snapped at him about staying on guard. I was being ungently marched back inside when Spelon returned and announced that everything seemed safe.

"You are positive?" Thal demanded.

"We have redone the scans and circled the perimeter," Spelon assured us. He lowered his pipe weapon and took a moment to tickle Thaarac's chin. Thaarac broke out into loud giggles and screams. Thal frowned at that, gave me a look, then waved Spelon away.

"All right," Thal said grudgingly. "Thedar, get a blanket for Thalia to sit on. Spelon, you stand first guard over the baby and Thalia. The rest of us can start camouflaging the ship. I do not want it visible from above."

The males worked for hours cutting down trees and dragging them over as Thal directed. With the use of the onboard computer, he constructed diagrams that showed angles and alignments of the foliage so they could best utilize the coverage but still allow a speedy takeoff if necessary.

Only when the males stopped for rests and for meals was I allowed to stand up and stretch. With Thaarac asleep on the blanket, having crawled about for hours to his great delight, I saw no reason why I couldn't help. Thal's response to my request was as grouchy as a Terran grizzly bear.

I kicked the dirt and then meandered about, picking up rocks and pieces of tree lichen, but even that brought growls from Thal, and he ordered me to behave.

"To a Warrior, idleness is more tiring than battle," Spelon said.

We all stared at him.

I think Thal was about to say something derogatory as soon as he could figure out exactly what Spelon meant. We all figured that Spelon, of all people, would never imply that I was a Warrior. But before Thal could question it, Spelon added, "I would be pleased to escort your wife for a small walk if you would trust me. It might allay her restlessness. I would not, of course, take her from your sight."

Thal eyed Spelon for a moment. The tension around us felt like everyone had suddenly forgotten how to exhale. I kept my eyes low and stayed out of it.

The silence continued so long that I wondered if the two of them would center off and do some nonfriendly wrestling. However, Thal surprised me (and, I think, the others). "You are right, Spelon. It is fitting you assume the responsibility of your position. Thalia belongs to me, and you are my Second.

"I shall acknowledge that. Tenor, Thedar, you are my witnesses. Spelon may take charge of Thalia in my absence. He is to have all the governance of her as needed. And, as Shaarvan desired, should I, for some unforeseeable reason, Pass to another Dimension, Thalia belongs to Spelon. Thank you, Spelon. You may walk Thalia about."

It was nothing new. Shaarvan had told me about that scenario back on Westla, but I wasn't crazy about the reminder of it.

"Thalia," Thal said, tapping my nose with his finger. "You will behave. I have just given Spelon the right to discipline as needed."

I was about to tell Thal that I'd be much happier sitting on my blanket when Spelon ordered me up. They were all staring at me, and Thal hadn't indicated I had a choice in the matter. I stood and walked to Spelon.

The shoes I had on were the good ones I'd engineered from the silly slippers the Shapechanger required females to wear, but even enhanced slippers were not what I'd recommend for hiking. The ground was thick with what looked like pine needles, and their needles invited themselves into my slippers to prick my toes and heels.

"You walk slowly, Thalia," Spelon complained.

I started to remind him that I wasn't a Warlord with long legs when I remembered the comment he'd made to Thal. Why had he said that? Why had Spelon come to my aid at all?

"You have my permission to talk, Thalia. What is your question?"

"How did you know . . . ?"

Spelon smiled down at me.

He never smiled. I bolted to a stop and stared.

"You must walk, or Thal will become angry, Thalia," Spelon warned.

I pulled a pine needle out of the top of my shoe and continued stepping forward. "Why did you offer to walk me, Spelon?"

"You were bored. I have noticed that you become troublesome when you are not given something to do."

"But why would. . ?"

"I rescind your permission to talk. Walk faster, Thalia. Soon, I must take you back."

We went as far as the edge of the forest. It was where the males were harvesting tree limbs for camouflage. I wanted to enter the forest, to walk between pines and sycamores, savoring their flavors. The breeze teased tauntingly. I inhaled deeply, breathing in the damp darkness, the pungent smell of lichen hanging from the fallen twigs and branches and on the ground, the soft matting of decaying bark. If only I could go just a little further . . . Spelon turned and began to walk back toward the ship. I sighed and followed.

"I knew you would like it," Spelon said. "The forest is inside you."

I stumbled, but Spelon didn't wait. I jogged to catch up.

Since when had Spelon become perceptive? Why had he taken me to the forest? Had he done it just to please me?

Spelon accompanied me to the edge of the blanket where I'd been before. My son was still sound asleep, lying next to Thedar. I thanked both males and sat.

The males, minus Tenor, whose turn it was to stand guard over Thaarac and me, worked until the last of the light was gone. Then, we all retreated back into the ship and spent the night inside its metal frame.

In the morning, Thal showed us a map of the ship's aerial surveillance. He had marked a place near our landing site that he thought would serve as our settlement. There was a stream nearby, and the forest would supply building materials. The others agreed.

Thal programmed the ship's materials we'd need. The ship issued them, and the males packed them into bags and strapped them on the auto-ground cart. The water, plant, and meat sources of the planet would provide us with our nutrients, all of which had been declared safe by the scout survey.

Thal also had suggestions about clothing requirements and articles to be brought individually. It was at that point that Spelon mentioned my shoes were not acceptable for the terrain.

After a moment's examination, Thal confirmed Spelon's appraisal. "I shall see to it that my wife's shoes are more appropriate. Thank you for your concern, Spelon. It is worthy of you."

It was strange how buddy-buddy the two of them were becoming when they had barely tolerated each other previously.

Due to all the preparations, when we finally walked down the ramp, the planet's sun was at quarter-rise, or midmorning as it would have been said on Earth. The Tide was pleasantly warm, and I was able to discard the coat that Thal had insisted I wear. Thaarac, too, did not need his outerwear, and I lightened his clothing. He seemed happy to rid himself of the bulkiness. It interfered with his ability to move rapidly — whether at a crawl or toddling about with his still shaky, slightly bowed legs.

Thaarac and I were, once again, required to stay on our blanket. I think my son didn't object to that as greatly as I did. He could at least occupy his time by stretching his limbs and attempting to crawl to the edge of the blanket before I pulled him back. But for me, the time was overly long. Tenor was posted as my guard, but he refused to talk with me while he was on duty. His stance was stern, and his eyes were vigilant. He kept the pipe ready to fire at all moments.

Nor was I permitted to make any noise. Only when I had to use the necessary did I brave enough to speak. Then, Tenor picked up Thaarac and escorted me back to the ship. When we returned, Thal stood on the ramp, his face livid, demanding to know why we'd returned to the ship. I was glad Tenor did the explaining.

"Thalia must get used to a lack of conveniences. She will use the ground from now on for her needs like the rest of us do," Thal ordered.

I looked around. There was no cover, no place to hide while I squatted. I decided not to drink a beverage at lunch break.

Thal noticed we were all pink from the sun. He went into the ship and came back out with a spray for our faces and hats for everyone. Thal sprayed me and tied the hat on my head. I felt like I was about Thaarac's age.

"It is my job to take care of you, Thalia. I shall do everything to protect you, regardless of my feelings or of yours. Remember that, my dear."

I thought Thal was talking about tying on my hat and sun-blocking my face, but I think he was already thinking about what was to come.

I was still staring after Thal, trying to make sense of his gloominess, when Spelon took my hand and, without asking Tren's permission, led me back down the path we had walked the Tide before. I gave him a big smile.

The new shoes that Thal had engineered were very much like Terran tennis shoes. It was easier for me to keep up with Spelon, and the pine needles didn't poke my feet anymore.

I thanked Spelon for speaking to Thal about it and told him how much more comfortable the new shoes were for walking. Spelon grunted, but I think he was pleased. He didn't seem to be in a talkative mood.

This time, Spelon took me further into the forest. I was delighted. The coolness inside and the damp, rich forest smell made for a pleasant walk. Spelon didn't have to be concerned about taking me out of Thal's sight. We both knew that Thal was walking behind us.

We stopped when we came to a slight clearing marked by four huge redwood trees. Spelon used his foot to clear an area of the larger pieces. I watched, wondering what he was doing. I was about to ask when he told me to lie down in the spot he'd prepared.

"Are you mad?" I said. "Thal would be furious. He . . ."

"I am Shapechanger, Thalia. Obey me."

Thal was close enough to hear our conversation. I was sure he'd come rushing up, demanding to know why we'd stopped. I also knew if I disobeyed Spelon, both Shapechanger would be angry with me. I lay down on the soft, decomposed bark and stared up at Spelon, mystified.

"I am your Second, Thalia. I am claiming you."

Claiming me? I hoped he didn't mean what I thought he did.

"Thal!" I called out, but although I could feel my husband's presence, he didn't come out from his hiding place.

Spelon's right hand held me down. With his other hand, he began to slide my dress upwards. Although I fought, I couldn't stop him. Spelon began to work patterns on my bare skin.

"No!" I cried, battling with his hands. "Thal," I screamed.

"Be silent, woman. Thal guards us. It is at his request that I claim you. Do not make it harder on him. What I do here must be done."

"No! You can't be my Second. Thal is my Second."

Spelon didn't answer me. Nor did Thal come rushing from his hiding place to save me. The patterns built up a stronger and stronger force. Spelon's Power was more potent than I'd supposed. I know I should have expected it. The strength of a male's Power determined whether he was a Warlord or not.

I'd struggled steadily up to that point with my hands, my body, and my mind, but when I realized the full extent of Spelon's Power, the fight went out of me, and my tears began. That didn't stop Spelon's patterns, either. The web grew tighter until I couldn't move. Then, Spelon's hand slid further down, touching me between my legs.

"Please don't do this, Spelon, Thal!" I cried out once more in a final, plaintive appeal.

The forest around us continued silent. The trees acted as sentinels, observing yet not involving themselves with Shapechanger matters. Somewhere in the low bushes all around us, Thal must be watching, standing guard over us. I sobbed louder, crushed by his treachery.

Spelon's finger slid into me. He didn't move it around. He did not intend it to be a pleasurable sensation for either of us. The solitary finger deep inside me gave him the contact he needed for the claiming. The webs strained as I fought against his Power, but it was already too late. The connection began our bonding cycle. No more than a sharp prick of pain, yet I sobbed — mainly from embarrassment.

When it was over, when my body had registered its new owner, Spelon pulled down my dress, rose up, and stared down at me. His eyes staggered me. His lust . . . Standing there on top of me, his legs on both sides of me, his erection pronounced, Spelon said, "You have felt my touch within you, Thalia. Should there be a need, you will accept my taking of you now. I am your Second, closest to your husband, Thal. You will obey me in all matters. You will look to me for guidance, and you will honor my bonds in all ways but those of a wifely nature."

The green light of Power eased from his eyes and seared the words into my brain. I breathed in huge gasps of air. The ache of the mind bond left a throbbing, burning headache. I could hear myself whimpering. I closed my eyes and tried to level out my breathing. I clenched my teeth to stop the pathetic mews that were still erupting from me. Apparently, I had no control over them.

Spelon released the web then and backed away. I felt him peering down at me, but I couldn't look at him. In a moment, he turned and left. Then, I was alone, fighting my emotional pain and tears. Alone if

I discounted the knowledge that all my bondmates were nearby and had sensed the bonding. Even with the lighter bonding I had with Tenor and Thedar, I could always feel their presence and emotions to some extent.

I curled up like a baby, breathing in hard, fast sobs. My tears of anger and fear were fading, and I was beginning to push down the memory in an attempt to pretend the bonding with Spelon hadn't happened. I thought about my visit with Brala and our discussion. What other choice did a woman have but to accept what the Shapechanger did to us when every rebellion was halted by a sharp word, a flash of a signal, or a look in their eyes?

Unless you were a Priestess. But how did that happen? How did one become a Priestess?

I sat up and hugged my knees to my face, wondering how long Thal would give me to recover. I was angrier with him than with Spelon. Couldn't Thal have warned me? Couldn't he have told me what was about to happen? Would that have made it easier or made any difference at all?

Spelon had done a good job preparing the ground beneath me. It was soft and fragrant. The smell of redwood permeated the air with its amazingly sweet scent. The four large redwoods, my sentinels, surrounded me and cradled me. I felt at home within their bower.

I was still crying off and on. I didn't hear Thal come up beside me. He sat and his arms gathered me to him.

"You take everything so hard, my dear," Thal said, rocking me back and forth. "Let it go. You are not hurt. Spelon did not discipline you when he could have. He was very gentle with you."

Didn't Thal know that Binding hurt? Even so, didn't he understand that my tears were not really about that, but the embarrassment of it, the unfairness, and the invasion? But Shapechanger males couldn't see through the eyes of a female.

"I don't understand how Spelon can be my Second. *You* are my Second," I said when I had stopped crying enough to get my voice back.

"Sh, my Thalia. Shapechanger always have a reason for what we do. You are a woman. You do not need to understand."

"Why?" I cried out, suddenly angry again.

"Careful, Thalia."

I knew the look in his eyes demanded caution. I swallowed my anger and breathed in the calmness of the redwoods.

Thal's hand caressed my face. "Good girl," he said. "You must remember, my Thalia, that all any of us do, we do to protect you. You are our treasure. That is all you need to know. Accept it. It is the Shapechanger way."

Thal's hand had slid to my jaw. He brought my chin up so he could study my eyes. I knew what he wanted. I nodded that I would not fight him. I was Shapechanger. I knew I had to accept.

Thal wrapped his own webs around me then and took me there in the forest. I wish I could say it was a romantic time, but even though I had nodded my compliance, there was still too much hurt and confusion in my brain to feel any passion. I think Thal believed I was fighting him, but I wasn't, or at least I didn't mean to. It was just that the memory of how he'd granted Spelon permission to touch me kept running through my mind, withering his webs.

When Thal had taken his pleasure and achieved mine, we walked back towards the others. I felt Spelon's presence following us. Had he stayed and watched Thal take me? My pride felt even more shredded.

I was sent to my place on the blanket, and Spelon and Thal went back to work, cutting down trees and dragging them to cover up the ship. Neither of them seemed to feel that there was any reason to converse more with me. I didn't want their presence, but their neglect of my feelings seemed even worse. I felt nauseated, watching them work side by side.

Thedar guarded Thaarac and me through the late afternoon. I sat quietly, half in shock, I think, trying to understand why Thal had believed I needed deeper binding with Spelon. Why had there been such an urge to label the backup of a backup? Did they believe that Shaarvan would never come for me? Did my bondmates think Thal's life was in danger? It angered me that all of them had participated in the act, either as witnesses or as participants.

And what was the point of bonding anyway? It was obvious Spelon could physically rape me whenever he wanted, despite the Shapechanger's aversion to such a thing. And Thal had never had a problem with it. Of course, Shapechanger did not consider being webbed the same as rape.

But I felt dirty. I wanted a water shower so badly I'd have chosen it over drink or food. But returning to the ship was not permitted. Thal had made that clear.

I had not drunk anything since the morning, but Thal's taking of me had made me feel the need to urinate. I held it in as long as I could, but as the sun lowered into the horizon, I could not ignore the urge any longer.

Thedar picked up a very wiggly Thaarac, led me about twenty paces from the ship, and ordered me to relieve myself.

"Will you promise to close your eyes? " I asked.

Thedar put Thaarac down on the ground at his feet and lifted up the pipe weapon. "I shall guard you as always, Thalia. My eyes will not be closed, but I shall be looking for enemies, not observing your ability to squat. I assume you will not need me to assist?"

I could not wait for another second. I pulled up my dress, crouched down, and peed. When I was done, Thedar tossed me a cloth, and I used it and returned it to him folded inward.

Without a word, Thedar picked up Thaarac, and we walked back to the blanket. Soon after that, Thaarac fell asleep. The evening began to cool. I covered my son with a blanket and then put on my coat. The sun gave off the loveliest colors as it sank under the horizon. As I watched, I reminisced over the many sunsets Shaarvan and I had seen from the wolf's lair, his arm around my shoulders, his lips plying my neck with kisses between strands of conversation. The forest there had breathed soft sighs, as this one did. A tear dangled on my eyelashes. I wiped it away.

As the sky grew grayer, the males dragged one more load. Thal ran a final computer scan using an almost invisible air drone that could show the ship from above and on all sides. The bondmates were pleased with the results. The camouflage looked complete.

By that time, the first stars had appeared. Thal pointed out the largest constellation and ordered everyone to take note of its position for future land navigation. Then we walked up the ramp and back onto the ship for what would be our last night aboard.

Thedar put Thaarac to bed, and I fled to the shower. The others gathered around the table and began celebrating. I rejoined them later, feeling considerably improved. Unfortunately, I discovered that while I'd been gone, Spelon and Thal had eaten little but celebrated a lot. He and Spelon were singing, waving their cups back and forth in time to their almost tuneless ditty. (I must admit that I have never heard a Shapechanger male sing in tune.)

I ate my dinner and waited, yawning steadily. Tenor stood and ordered me to leave with him. I looked at Thal for permission, but he was still singing. I think he'd forgotten me.

Tenor slid his hand about my neck to end my indecision. I figured he was returning me to my room, but instead, he took me to his.

When the door slid open, I argued. The neck grip tightened and Tenor half pushed, half carried me inside. My heart jumped throat-ward. I thought it must be Tenor's turn to claim me. Maybe, I was just being passed around! I felt sick.

Tenor told me to use the necessary and then to get into his bed. I obeyed the part about using the necessary room. But once inside, I was too cowardly to come out, and Tenor had to issue a Shapechanger command to eject me.

I didn't remove my dress before I got into bed. It was a bit rebellious of me, but Tenor didn't comment. He smoothed the covers over me, bent down to kiss me on the forehead, and said, "Pretend that I am your brother tonight, little one. You are Thal's. You must trust that I would never dishonor that. I brought you here only because it will be safer for you. Sleep now, Thalia. Tomorrow, we must walk far."

Then he backed away and sat down in the chair beside the bed. I knew by that and his words that I was safe.

"Thank you, Tenor," I whispered and closed my eyes.

Chapter Seven

Tren, on the artificial planet, Westla

Transition is a strange process. They said I had completed it during my deep sleep time, but they were wrong. Each Tide, I woke up and discovered something else I hadn't known.

My hearing was such that unidentified sounds clanged and thumped from every side of me. It was quite disturbing. Even the air ventilation system droned with a noise that I found semi-deafening. Whispers from rooms far away pestered me. Stray thoughts barraged my brain. I couldn't tune them out, and their clamor was a constant downpour on my mind.

The smells that rode the air circuits were murmurs of their own sort. Flavors, both tasteful and objectionable, were a constant assault. My mind attempted to separate and label them while the Old Ones kept up the spiel of information they were ramming down my throat.

Only Lyda kept me sane. Without her companionship, her generous body, and her sweet kisses, the battering would have beaten me down. I savored her warmth. The smell and taste of her was an added pleasure.

The Old Ones allowed me to move into a suitable apartment. It adjoined the hospital and lab, but its insulation from the chaos around me helped. My senses were still constantly being attacked, but to a lesser degree, and the privacy of the new dwelling was calming. Its separation from the medical atmosphere of poking needles and doctor consultations restored me almost as much as Lyda.

From my new home, I was also free to journey out and explore Westla. I accepted some of the invitations I had been given. I skied with Gres and his wife. I swam in a clear-water lake. I took in shows and toured galleries. And I continued with the Old Ones, training, training, and training.

Tessa, the Head High Priestess, came to visit me. She was Shaara's guide, she told me.

"How is Shaara?" I asked immediately, but the old witch avoided my question so adeptly I did not realize it until she had left.

I hunted the woman down at her residence and demanded to see her, but her door stayed closed to me. Why had she teased me? Why had she told me that she was Shaara's guide if she would not speak of my . . . my sister?

A sevenTide passed. I was still in training. Targone returned to Freinana. He had visited me often. I missed his friendship. A link to one's home is hard to give up.

I wanted to learn more about the Priestess. I was curious yet still angry with her. I questioned the Old Ones until they became irritated with my persistence and sent me away. I had long ago learned they would not speak of Shaara. It seemed that Tessa was another subject on which they would give me no enlightenment.

I researched, questioned Tem, and from my new friends, gathered up an education about the etiquette of a Shapechanger in the presence of a Priestess. Several Tides later, with improved manners and my new knowledge of protocol, I once more set out to approach Tessa in her home.

"I greet you with honor, Priestess Tessa," I said at her doorway.

She cackled loudly but permitted my entrance. It was a successful visit in everything except my queries of Shaara. Not a word passed Tessa's lips concerning my former Freinanan slave. Nor would Tessa discuss the whereabouts of Shaarvan. It puzzled me. Was I not the Lord's brother? Had it not been by his request that I had been forced into transition? Yet Shaarvan had not visited me once, nor had I been able to find out where he lived. That also puzzled me.

Tessa was an odd one, for sure. Her tongue was sharper than a silver *proboscis lizard's*. Her brain was quick and agile. I could tell she enjoyed my company. In fact, she was even the smallest bit flirtatious. I grew tired of the visit before she did. As I left, the cackle of her laughter echoed in my ears.

Thalia, on the planet Deadstar

As could be expected, there was a disturbance in the night. Thal started banging on the door and kept it up until he was finally admitted. Then, he began to yell and throw punches at Tenor.

"You stole my wife!" Thal kept thundering.

I was quivering under the blankets. I would have defended Tenor, but he had issued the silence command, so I lay as still as possible and pretended to be asleep.

Tenor did not seem to need my help. He decked Thal with a couple of punches that would have made Spelon proud. Then he straightened

Thal's legs out, threw a blanket over him, and ordered me to go back to sleep.

"You're going to leave Thal there?" I questioned, hoping that the silence command would no longer hold.

"It will allay his jealousy if he realizes he slept in the same room with you, Thalia, but he is still too drunk for me to leave you alone with him.

"Tomorrow, we shall all have to be very calm and subdued. I suspect that both Spelon and Thal will require a full measure of *Burbwel* and a morning of silence."

"Thank you, Tenor," I whispered. "I am sorry I was difficult last night."

"I understand. Spelon claimed you. You are distrustful of us again. Do not be, Thalia. You must have faith in all your bondmates. We would never hurt you — not unnecessarily."

I sat up and pulled the covers higher. "Why did Spelon do that? I do not understand. Thal is my Second. Why did . . ."

"Thal is your husband. It is his right to assign a Second."

"Do you and Thedar agree with it?"

"Go to sleep, Thalia."

"Meaning you don't want to talk about it?"

Tenor flashed the obey command. I sighed. Tenor lay down on top of the blankets. His arms surrounded me and pulled me close, but I did not fear him then. I sighed once more and closed my eyes.

When I woke the next morning, Tenor signaled silence. I tiptoed over Thal and showered and dressed. When we left, Thal was still snoring up a gale.

Thedar joined us in a few minutes, bringing Thaarac. The three of us ate our breakfast while we fed and chatted with the toddler. Then, we waited and waited. Thedar and Tenor began to play a card game. They would not include me, but I was free to watch. They attempted to show Thaarac how to play. He liked the attention, but, of course, he didn't understand the game. Mostly, he just drooled on the cards.

Thal was the first to wake up. He came in red-eyed and irritable. "Come here, Thalia," he demanded, and I obeyed promptly.

His arm circled me, and he pulled me close and kissed my cheek. "Did Tenor take you last night?" he whispered harshly in my ear.

"No!" I cried out, horrified by the suggestion.

"Sh," Thal ordered, closing his eyes against the pain.

"Did he touch you in any way, Thalia?" Thal asked, putting his finger to my lips.

That was a silent command. I nodded my head, knowing Thal would not accept even the slightest lie.

"Whisper your answer, Thalia. Where did he touch you?"

"He used the neck grip to walk me to his room, and then he kissed me goodnight on the forehead, and, later, when you were there, he lay on top of the cover and held me through the night."

"Thank you, Thalia. Go sit over there," he said, pointing to the bench on the other wall.

Thal walked over to the two males and talked quietly with Tenor. Thedar brought Thal a drink. I wondered if it was the *Burbwell* Tenor had spoken of before.

Spelon came stumbling in soon after. He looked like he was ready to eat someone. I was glad I was sitting clear across the room. Thedar got up and brought him a drink, also.

By the time the two males were more their normal hue, both Thaarac and my bottom were asleep. I began to fidget, wanting desperately to be allowed up. Either my movement or my thoughts drew Thal's eyes.

"You may get up, Thalia, but be quiet. Thedar, would you take Thaarac back to the playroom and let him crawl around? We shall not be disembarking this Tide. It would not be safe with two of us feeling ill. We shall set out in the nextTide."

"Could Tenor, Thedar, and I go for a walk outside?" I asked with a voice scarcely above a whisper. Even so, Thal winced.

"No. You will not leave the ship without me, Thalia." The eyes that looked my way were red as the cradle berries on Freinana.

For the rest of the Tide, the ship was very quiet. I picked up a book from one of the tables in Thal's research room and attempted to learn more about quasars. Even so, Thal repeatedly complained about my restlessness, yet he wouldn't allow me to leave.

Spelon apparently spent most of the Tide working out on the wrestling mats. Thal joined him later. Thedar, who stopped by for a few minutes to watch them, told me that working out as they were doing was the best way for males to get rid of the poisons they'd imbibed. But when I asked him why they had gotten drunk in the first place, he just smiled.

That night, I slept with Thal, and the next morning, everything was back to normal. Thal shut down most of the ship's components, except for the health monitor, which ran checks on each of us each Tide, and the surveillance alert, which would inform us of any approaching vessels.

The males heaved packs containing food and anything else they wanted that hadn't fit on the already overfull landwalker. Then we began our journey.

We traveled through the forest where Spelon and I had gone a twoTides before. Thal had shuffled the redwood chips back into position before we'd left, and there were many small clearings with four sentinels, so I could only guess at the site. Maybe that was a good thing since I had very bitter memories of it.

We walked for a long time underneath the redwoods, and my arms ached from carrying Thaarac. No matter how I shifted him about, he felt heavy and awkward. Spelon came over and took the baby from me.

"Already she grows tired," Spelon informed Thal.

"I'm OK," I snapped, drawing scowls from both males.

We continued on for hours. My legs had been fine on the ship. I'd walked and jogged often there, but this soft, chip-filled, and dust-heavy surface was straining muscles I'd never felt before. I began to stumble, in spite of the new shoes I wore. Thal called for a rest.

When we sat down, Thal rubbed my calves and thighs. It embarrassed me. No one else seemed to be suffering from the long hike. Thal handed me a drink and a bar of something sweet and sour. It had a strange taste, but it took away some of my tiredness. I noticed that everyone was eating the same thing. Even Thaarac had been given a bite of it after Thal had first chewed it into a mash.

When my bondmates stood up, I wasn't ready to continue, but Thal had given the order, so we must. I watched the males place the heavy packs on their backs. Spelon wore the largest and also carried my son. My respect for the males' strength humbled me. I vowed that no matter how tired I became, I wouldn't complain.

We continued on, stepping over fallen logs and through banks of ferns and occasional creeks, which we had to hop across or drag logs over to create a passage. The landwalker, with all the building materials (and mainly Thal's books,) jetted across, but its solar battery was limited. Thal worried that too many creek crossings would necessitate stopping until it recharged.

I would have enjoyed our trek if the males had all slowed down. But my legs were cramping worse, and each step was becoming an agony.

"Tenor, lift her up and unto my back. She has had enough," Thal said at one point.

I was so tired by then that I didn't even react to the order. With my arms around Thal's neck and my legs around his waist, we walked on. And when Thal tired, the packs were shifted, and each of my bondmates carried me in such a fashion, except Spelon, who refused to give up his pack. He carried me in his arms with his heavy pack, bowing him low.

"I didn't ask to be carried," I told Spelon when he made a comment to the others about my lack of stamina.

"Of course, you did not. You are a Warrior," he said and kissed my arm.

That shut me up faster than a silence command. Since when had Spelon been allowed to bestow kisses?

I clamped down on all my thoughts and watched the scenery.

It was after a quick lunch and several afternoon breaks that we finally reached the other side of the forest. Thedar was carrying me then, but I felt rested and wanted to walk. Thal had jogged on ahead to scout out the trail, so I couldn't ask him for permission. Ignoring Spelon's warning that I would hold them back, Thedar permitted me to walk again.

I have spoken little of Thedar, yet he was a favorite of mine — for his wisdom and gentleness and because I believe he always saw me as a person, not just a female. Thedar was just as mighty a Warrior as the others, but he was not prone to argumentativeness or spurious decisions. I suppose he was the peacemaker of the group, although Tenor wasn't fond of disagreements either.

In appearance, Thedar was lithe but well-muscled and as handsome as all Shapechanger. He had dark, serious eyes that recorded and analyzed everything adroitly, which is why, although Spelon had the right to prevent my walking, the others were prone to listen to Thedar's words. Because Thedar allowed it, I was once more free to move about.

We had left the giant trees and found ourselves in a wooded area. The ground beneath us was filled with more dirt and rocks than pine needles and chunks of bark. Some of the trees held fruits and nuts that dangled from their branches. I wondered if we could eat them. Thedar didn't know. He said later we could scan them.

The woods were filled with a soft, decomposing layer of leaves and squishy fruit. It made for slippery walking and forced us to move with slightly pigeon-footed steps. Tenor fell down once, and Spelon yanked him back up. The heavy padding of leaves at least had softened Tenor's fall.

Spread over the rotting underside were fresh fallen leaves. We were apparently in autumn on this side of the planet. The leaves on the trees and on the ground held golds, oranges, and mustardy yellows. I loved the sound as we tramped through them — the crackling as our shoes crushed their dried-up skeletons.

The smell was heavenly, too. One kind of tree was dripping sap that smelled exactly like maple syrup. Spelon complained, grumbling about the stench robbing his hunter's nose, but I smiled, remembering Saturday morning waffles with my parents.

The woods were warmer than the forest had been. The faces of the males began to drip with sweat. I, too, felt sticky, even though I was not burdened with heavy packs or the weight of my son, who was at that moment being carried by Spelon.

We saw our first wild animal in the woods. It was striped like a zebra but with short legs and the long-haired beard of a Billy goat. Spelon raised his pipe and shot. I was glad he missed it.

Thal returned shortly after that. Across his back was the animal we'd seen, or one like it. Thal's eyes scanned me, then Thaarac. He called for a break, and we practically dropped in place. The males built a fire and began to cook the poor, dead animal. I had my hands full with Thaarac, who seemed determined to waddle his way to the fire or, perhaps, the animal he saw there. Thaarac fussed and fought me until Spelon strode over and picked him up.

"A Shapechanger heeds his mother, Thaarac. You may not go closer to the fire. It would cause you great pain."

He put Thaarac down, and my son immediately stuck his finger in his mouth and stared up at Spelon with enormous eyes. He wasn't frightened by the huge Shapechanger as much as pensive. I think he was thinking over what Spelon had said. I wasn't sure that he was old enough to analyze such a statement, but Thaarac didn't insist on crawling towards the fire again.

At first, I refused to eat the cooked meat, but Thal handed me a chunk, and I was told to eat it. I chewed and swallowed, feeling sorry for the pretty little animal, but I had to admit that it was delicious.

While we ate, Thal talked about what he'd seen. Beyond the woods were fields with rich grass and abundant flowers but no protection for camouflage. Thal told the others that we must build our houses concealed within the woods. It would be the safest place for us.

We went no further that evening. We bedded down, body next to body. Thal did not take me that night. I was very relieved since the others were all nestled so close. In the morning, when I woke, I found that Tenor and Thedar had slipped away. They had set out to scout the area for the best place to build our housing. We breakfasted on Stubra meat, which is what Thal told us the animal had been named by the original survey team.

Not until Tenor and Thedar returned did we journey on. They had found the perfect spot, they told us. A stream brought fresh water to a small vale, and there were lovely trees all around. And, best of all, they said that we did not have far to go.

Later, Spelon caught four stubras in traps he had laid. He wove ropes from the inner side of the reeds around the stream and fastened the ropes around the captured stubras' necks. Like dogs on leashes, they followed Spelon submissively.

I was ecstatic when Spelon gave them over to my care. Within minutes, I had made friends with them. They responded quickly to my petting and handfeeding and were so happy with all the attention they were soon put to work. They proved to be stronger than their size denoted, and by evening, the stubras were actually pulling the huge tree trunks needed to construct our first dwelling.

I had never seen a house constructed, and I was curious. I wasn't sure that my bondmates knew what they were doing, but Thal had experience from his travels. He directed the males to pour a cement mixture he'd brought from the ship. It formed the floor of the house.

The tree trunks were placed upright into this mixture, forming a four-sided fence-like structure in the shape of a huge rectangle. A second mixture was added. It bubbled like yeast and rose up over and around the tree trunks, forming a seal. As the mixture darkened, it coated everything and turned into a lovely oak color.

I was curious what Thal would do for a roof, but the sky grew dark, and for another night, we slept outside under the stars.

Earlier, Spelon had sat Thaarac on the back of the smallest animal, holding him securely as he walked forward. Ever since, Thaarac had been captivated. That night, as we sat around the campfire, Thaarac said his first word — Stub, and he pointed to where the animals were tied. Of course, he got a lot of attention for it and by the time he was yawning and rubbing his eyes, he was saying a perfectly clear *stubra.*

Thal did not abstain that night but carried me a short distance from the others. He used his webs and patterns, but he probably didn't need them anymore. My body had adapted and now craved his touch.

Afterward, we rejoined the others, and a few moments later, I noticed Spelon slipping back into our circle of bodies. It was embarrassing to realize he had stood guard for us.

The fire's uneven whispering, the crackling of the logs falling into the flame, the night sounds that were unfamiliar, and at least three Shapechanger males lying close to me, all of whom snored loudly, could have caused the night to last over long. But, amazingly, in

Thal's arms with Spelon's or another of the male's eyes on watch throughout the night, I slept deeply.

The next morning, Thal instructed us on the proper procedure to install a roof. Basically, it was much like the previous Tide's work. Tree trunks were cut horizontally and fitted on top of the walls, planking across the top like bridges between a canyon's cliffs. When these thin-cut trunks all covered the roof, again, the fizzy stuff was used. It bubbled, yeasted, and coated until the whole building looked like a giant brown gift box.

I was wondering how we were supposed to get inside since the giant sugar cube of a rectangle had no openings — neither door nor windows. I was pretty sure, also, that since there was no avenue for light, the inside must be like a night sky without stars.

I should have known that Thal would have the answer to such problems. A tool that looked similar to the pipe weapons the males carried carved out a door and four windows. Another chemical was used to spray the windows with a clear substance. This plastic-like material, when it was finished, had the appearance of pineapple lifesavers cooked in an oven. Light streamed in abundantly, and Thal said the surface would be thoroughly watertight.

Thal put on hinges for the door he'd cut into a section of the wall, and then he fastened room dividers from sections of tree limbs and another round of chemical paste. That constituted the partitions for the kitchen and bedroom. I marveled at all the things Thal knew how to do and realized Shaarvan had not just chosen Thal to be my husband because he owned an escape ship and was a super smart astronomer.

Thal and I did not spend that night under the stars. I do not know where the others slept, but we were in our bedroom, atop and under piles of soft, cushioned blankets.

In the morning, the males began the construction of a second building, which was to house them. While it was being built, Thal took time to start a garden. He used a stubra to plow a surface with a sharpened tree limb and then helped me to gather up the grass and weeds, which were tossed to the side to become the start of our compost heap. Spelon came over, too, and began to work. Then, soon, the others drifted over, which meant that their house would not be finished for another couple of Tides. The males said they didn't care.

Taking advantage of their enthusiasm, Thal had them help him with a waterway. It connected the stream with the garden so water could be directed in and out. The males finished plowing the entire garden and dug half the waterway. They worked long into the evening. When they stopped, we ate by the light of the fire, feasting on ship food and leftover stubra.

In a fiveTide, Thal gave me seeds for the vegetable garden. I had planted a garden long ago when I was growing up in California. This one was no different, except that the seeds had strange labels, and I couldn't read the package directions. Thal had to tell me how deep to plant each type of seed.

Shaarac loved the garden. He crawled about in the soft dirt and seemed to taste each area. I was constantly removing dirt and twigs from his mouth. When the waterway opened and the water flowed in, I scooped Shaarac up and held him, although he screamed to be put back down.

The garden was given to me as my chore. I was to weed and water it. Spelon argued with that, saying that taking care of the stubras and the garden was too much for me. But I was delighted. It was good to feel useful.

Tenor or Spelon chose to hunt animals and bring the kill back to the house. Thal taught me how to clean the carcasses and prepare them for our meals. That was not a chore I enjoyed, but I worked at Thal's side, and it went quickly. We buried the parts of the animal we didn't use in the garden. Thal said it would improve the soil.

I was becoming quite accomplished with my butchering, and I even learned how to dry the meat and help Thal prepare it in different ways. But, about a twelveTide after our arrival, the sight of the dead thing, dripping with blood, forced me to run into the bushes and vomit all that I had eaten.

When I was emptied, I returned to my bondmates on very shaky feet. I kept trying to remember if I'd inadvertently told a lie, but I couldn't think of anything. Shapechanger never get sick. My flu symptoms made no sense.

Thal had moved the stubra carcass away, but the memory of it still made me gag. When I saw the spot where we usually prepared the meat, I turned and sank to the ground, not even able to crawl away. It didn't matter. I had nothing left to throw up.

After a moment, Thal handed me a cup of water and patted my back. I rinsed my mouth and, lying in the dirt, waited to see if the nausea continued. When the dry heaves seemed to be over, I looked up at Thal and said, "I didn't tell a fib."

"I know," he said softly.

I sat up and watched an earthworm wiggling in the soil where Thaarac had just plowed with his stick. The worm was squirming side to side, digging itself back into the soil. What did you call an earthworm on Deadstar? A dead starworm?

Thedar showed Thaarac a pile of oblong creek rocks he'd brought him. The burly Warrior sat down on the ground and slowly counted rocks out loud. "One, two, three . . ." he said, as Thaarac watched.

Thal stooped down and lifted me up. "We must talk," he said and he carried me over to an old log the others had placed by the house.

I cast a quick look over at my son, checking that Thedar was still with him. I tried not to take my eyes off Thaarac — ever. The toddler had no fear of anything and always seemed to head for danger, but Thedar was still sitting beside him, counting rocks and teaching my son how to stack them.

I drew in a few rather unsure breaths, but I was feeling better. Thal, sitting beside me, raised my hand to his mouth and kissed it. For a moment, we both watched Thedar playing with Thaarac.

I'd thought Thal had said that we must talk, but so far, he had done nothing more than clear his throat. I cast my glance about the clearing. The stubras were grazing nearby. Spelon had roped off a section of the yard for them. They could have ducked under or even pushed the rope down, but they didn't. I think they liked being near us. They had grown even more friendly now that they'd learned to appreciate being petted and having their itchy foreheads scratched.

"Thalia," Thal began finally. "Thaarac needs a brother."

Thaarac seemed as happy as a *tidle bug* savoring a pile of manure. "I think he's fine, Thal. He has all of you to entertain him."

"No. He needs a brother."

I sighed and looked up at Thal's face. "If you're asking if I want another baby, the answer is 'no.' I'm never going through pregnancy again. It makes me fat and miserable, and the delivery is painful."

Thal reached out and took my other hand. The largeness of his when it covered mine always shocked me. Thal was not as huge as my other bondmates, but he had the biggest hands and feet. Thal's eyes grew more serious like he had something important to tell me or like he was worried about something.

"I am going about this poorly, Thalia," he said. "I am not asking you. That is not the Shapechanger way. A male chooses and executes. I decided on Westla that you would give Thaarac a brother."

"You mean, you're going to force me to have your child?"

He shook his head but avoided my eyes, looking out across the woods, where the trees were shedding leaves in an array of colors. "I mean, I impregnated you on Westla."

The air around me froze at the word *impregnated.* Past tense. As in, Thal had already done it.

"No!" I cried out, jerking my hands away so I could flee from his words.

"Sit down, Thalia," he ordered. I dropped back onto the log and searched his eyes, hoping desperately that this was just some odd little joke he was playing on me.

"Please, tell me you didn't. It was awful last time. Thaarac was too big, and he didn't want to come out!"

"It will be your second baby, Thalia. It will not be as hard."

That explained the nausea — morning sickness — the quirky part of having once been human. I remembered how sick I'd been with Shaarac and how Shaarvan had . . .

"What will Shaarvan say?" There was panic in my voice. I should have modulated it, but the alarm I felt was a bursting dam.

"He will say it is my right."

Thal's eyes clouded like the sun's warmth had gone beyond the mountains and left only the night's chilly air. Speaking of Shaarvan always seemed to irritate Thal, so I rarely spoke my husband's name anymore, even though I was still his. How could I be pregnant with another man's child?

Thaarac was singing to his sticks. His song was as off-key as the other males' voices always were. Did he not hear the lack of melody?

I felt another wave of nausea. I gagged and launched my body back down to the ground. Thal caught me and held me still. "Breathe in, Thalia. Breathe deeply."

I wanted to die — and he was telling me to breathe? I took in air and held it. Thal's hands still clenched my arms. If I threw up, he would be drenched. I wanted to ask him to free me, but I couldn't speak. Breathe in. Hold. Breathe in. Hold.

The nausea passed after a moment. I opened my eyes. Thal's eyes were still fastened on mine. He was waiting for me to say something. He was waiting for my acceptance.

How could Thal have done this to me? How could he have felt that my body was his to use in such a way? I was Shaarvan's. It was Shaarvan's right, not Thal's.

Thal was still waiting and obviously not picking up my thoughts. "Good girl," he said, which I assumed was for not throwing up again.

Didn't he know how I hated that? I wanted to throw his arms off me, to scream, to hit him, to cry. I did none of those.

Thal took a cloth and wiped my face. The dampness cooled me. I had not realized how hot I was. Thal urged me to drink again. I sipped at the water he handed me.

I looked down at my stomach. I was still flat. How far along was I? Thal had said he'd planted me in Westla. Was that a twentyTide or a thirtyTide ago?

"Why haven't I been sick before?" I asked.

"The ship monitored your body. It supplied all your needs, Thalia. Apparently, it was able to keep the Terran sickness away until now."

I sighed with irritation. Shaarvan had once explained that Shapechanger males were always fertile when they chose to be, and being in the zone, or whatever they called it, pulled the female's egg into position. So, there it was — a done deal. How had Thal put it — he decided, then executed. Simple, for him.

I had never thought about having another child. If the war on Altar had not come, I suppose Shaarvan would have seeded me again. I knew he'd wanted more sons. If it had been up to me . . . But I was a Shapechanger. It had never been my decision.

With my sigh, Thal relaxed and stretched out his hand to play with a lock of my hair. I had not given him my acceptance, but then he hadn't asked.

"I must go prepare the kill, Thalia," he said gently after a few minutes passed in silence. "You will be excused from that chore from now on. I am sorry about the morning sickness. I thought it would not plague you since you are fully Shapechanger. I do not have the drug to stop it."

He stood up, kissed my head, and walked away. I sat there, watching him. His long legs ate up any distance. A small leaf, driven by the breeze, had fallen onto his shoulder. As his arms swung back and forth in rhythm with his muscled thighs, the leaf slid down the back of his shirt, twirled in the air, then glided gently to fall to the ground.

There should be a metaphor for falling leaves and my situation. Was it inevitability, nature having a good laugh, or just the reality that when things are okay, something always made them worse? Probably, it was Freida's god interfering again, but that had nothing to do with leaves.

I walked over to the garden and opened the sluice for more water. Thal had told me the seeds I'd planted were a special kind, bio-something that would be eatable in a seven Tide. I had trouble believing that, but if Thal said it would happen that quickly, I knew it would.

I didn't know how Shapechanger activated their sperm. Did they have an on-off switch in their brains? Did they say *impregnate*, and it immediately happened?

Thal's words opened a memory I'd long ago buried. Like in a dream, like it happened to someone else, I heard Tessa telling Thal to plant his seed. Then I remembered the snow. I knew why Thal had done it. I also understood why my body accepted Thal's demands so readily. It had been Tessa who'd told Thal how to break down my resistance.

I pulled a couple of weeds from the garden, using my bare hands, even though Thal had told me not to. He'd given me gloves and ordered me to always wear them when I gardened. But the gloves were inside, and I'd have to pass Thal preparing the kill. I couldn't face that, nor did I feel in the mood to see him.

I supposed it was kind of ludicrous. Thal had put me in charge of two gardens and had supplied the seeds for both. My tears started as I pulled up another of the weeds.

The Shaarvan Series continues with:

Book Six

No Longer Shaara of Shaarvan

www.ingramcontent.com/pod-product-compliance
Lightning Source LLC
Chambersburg PA
CBHW071328250626
47159CB00004B/1510